The Last Witness

Also by K. J. Parker

The Fencer Trilogy
Colours in the Steel
The Belly of the Bow
The Proof House

The Scavenger Trilogy
Shadow
Pattern
Memory

The Engineer Trilogy
Devices and Desires
Evil for Evil
The Escapement

The Company
The Folding Knife
The Hammer
Sharps
Purple and Black
Blue and Gold
Savages

The Two of Swords
Academic Exercises (collection)

As Tom Holt
(selected titles)
Expecting Someone Taller
Who's Afraid of Beowulf?
Flying Dutch
Faust Among Equals
Snow White and the Seven Samurai
Valhalla
The Portable Door
You Don't Have to Be Evil to Work Here, But It Helps
The Better Mousetrap
Blonde Bombshell
The Outsorcerer's Apprentice
Holt! Who Goes There? (collection)

THE LAST WITNESS

K. J. Parker

A TOM DOHERTY ASSOCIATES BOOK

NEW YORK

THE LAST WITNESS

A Tor.com Book

Published by Tom Doherty Associates, LLC

175 Fifth Avenue

New York, NY 10010

www.tor.com

Tor® is a registered trademark of Tom Doherty Associates, LLC.

ISBN 978-1-4668-9348-1 (e-book)

ISBN 978-0-7653-8529-1 (trade paperback)

First Edition: October 2015

The Last Witness

I remember waking up in the middle of the night. My sister was crying. She was five years old, I was eight. There was a horrible noise coming from downstairs, shouting, banging. We crept to the top of the stairs (really it was just a glorified ladder) and I peered down. I couldn't see all that well, because the fire had died down and the lamps weren't lit. I saw my father; he'd got his walking stick in his hand, which was odd because why would he need it indoors? My mother was yelling at him; you're stupid, you're so stupid, I should have listened to my family, they said you were useless and you are. Then my father swung the stick at her. I think he meant to hit her head, but she moved and he caught her on the side of the left arm. Oddly, instead of backing away she went forward, toward him. He staggered and fell sideways, onto the little table with the spindly legs; it went crunch under his weight, and I thought; he's broken it, he's going to be in so much trouble. Then my sister screamed. My mother looked up at us, and I saw the knife in her hand. She yelled, "Go to *bed*!" She yelled at us all the time. We were always getting under her feet.

I also remember a night when I couldn't sleep. I was about six. Mummy and Daddy were having a horrible row downstairs, and it made me cry. I cried so much I woke up my brother. Forget it, he told me, they're always rowing, go to sleep. I couldn't stop crying. Something bad's going to happen, I said. I think he thought so too, and we crept to the top of the stairs and looked down, the way we used to spy on the guests-for-dinner. I saw Daddy knock Mummy to the ground with his stick, and then Uncle Sass (he wasn't really our uncle) jumped out from behind the chimney corner and stabbed Daddy with a knife. Then Mummy saw us and yelled at us to go back to bed.

I also remember the night my husband died.

I remember that job very clearly.

———————

I remember, when I was growing up, we lived on the edge of the moor, in a little house in a valley. About five miles north, just above the heather-line, were these old ruins. I used to go there a lot when I was a boy. Mostly the grass had grown up all over them, but in places the masonry still poked out, like teeth through gums. It must have been a big city once—of course, I didn't know about cities then—and there was this tall square pillar; it stood about ten feet and it was leaning slightly. Between the wind and the rain and the sheep itching against it, there wasn't much left to see of the carvings; rounded outlines that were probably meant to be people doing things, and on one side, where the slight lean sheltered it a tiny bit from the weather, there were these markings that I later realised must have been writing. I can picture them in my mind to this day; and when I became rich and had some spare time I searched the Studium library, which is the finest in the world (the memory of the human race, they call it) but I never found anything remotely like that script, or any record of any city on our moors, or any race or civilisation who'd ever lived there.

———————

I remember the first time I met them. When you've been in this business as long as I have, clients tend to merge together, but these ones stand out in my mind. There was an old man and a younger one; father and son or uncle and nephew, I never did find out. The old man was big, broad and bony, with a long face and a shiny dome of a head, nose like a hawk's beak, very bright blue sunken eyes, big ears sticking out like handles. The young man was just like him only red-haired and much smaller; you could have fitted him comfortably inside the old man, like those trick dolls from the East. He didn't talk much.

We heard all about you, the old man said, the stuff you can do. Is it true?

Depends what you've heard, I told him. Most of what people say about me is garbage.

I think he expected me to be more businesslike. Is it true, he said, that you can read people's minds?

No, I told him, I can't do that, nobody can, not even the Grand Masters. That would be magic, and there's no such thing. What I can do (I said quickly, before I tried his patience too far) is get inside people's heads and take their memories.

They both looked at me. That's what we'd heard, the old man said, but we weren't sure if we could believe it. And anyhow, isn't that mind reading?

So many of them say that. I don't know how I do it, I told them, and neither does anyone else. None of the professors at the Studium could explain it. According to them, it's not possible. All I know is, I can see my way into someone's head—literally, I stare at him hard, and the wall of his skull seems to melt away, and then it seems to me that I'm standing in a library. On three sides of me there are shelves, floor to ceiling, spaced about nine inches apart; on the shelves are thousands and thousands of scrolls of parchment, like in the Old Library at Marshand. Each scroll is in a brass cylinder, with a number and the first line of the text embossed on the cap. Don't ask me how, but I know what's in each one. I reach out my hand—I actually have to lift my arm and reach out physically—and it seems to me that I pull down the scroll I want from the shelf and unscrew the cap; then I walk over to the window (there's always a window) because the light's better there, and there's a chair. I sit down and unroll the scroll and look at it, at which point the memory becomes mine, just exactly as though it had happened to me. Then I roll up the scroll and put it under my arm; the moment I've done that, the whole illusion fades, I'm back where I started, and no time has passed. The memory stays in my head, but the client or the victim will have forgotten it completely and forever; won't even remember that he ever had that memory to begin with, if you see what I mean. Anyway, I said, that's what I do. That's all I can do. But I'm the only man alive who can do it, and as far as I know, nobody's ever been able to do it before.

The old man was dead quiet for maybe five heartbeats, and his face was frozen. And you do this for money? he said.

I nodded. For a great deal of money, yes.

I could see he didn't believe me. That's pretty remarkable, he said, and it does sound quite a lot like magic. Is there any way—?

I can prove it? I gave him my unsettling grin. Sure, I said. I can't prove it to you, of course, but I can prove it, to someone else who you trust. I'll have to damage you a bit, I'm afraid. Up to you.

He actually went pale when I said that. He asked me to explain, so I did. I told him, think of a memory you share with someone else. I'll take that memory out of your head. Then I'll describe it, and the person you shared it with will confirm that it's authentic. Of course, you'll have forgotten it forever, so please choose something you don't particularly value.

He gave me that horrified look. You're sure you don't read minds, he said. I told him, I was sure. Can't be done, I told him. Not possible.

Well, he whispered with the young man for a moment or so, and then he told me about an afternoon in early autumn, twenty years ago. A boy falls out of an apple tree and cuts his forehead. He starts crying, and the noise disturbs an old black sow asleep in the shade; the sow jumps up and trots away snorting; the boy stops crying and laughs.

I recited what he'd told me back to him, slowly and carefully. He gives me a worried grin. Will it hurt? He's joking. I nod, tell him I'm afraid so, yes. Before he can answer, I'm inside his head.

(This is where I'm uncertain. What I see, every time

14

I go through, is always the same. It's very much like the Old Library at the Studium, except that the shelves are a much darker wood—oak, I think, rather than red cedar—and the window is to the left, not the right, and the ceiling has plaster mouldings, but vine and grape clusters rather than geometric patterns, and the line of the floorboards is north-south, not east-west. Maybe it's just that my mind has taken the Old Library as a sort of template and embellished it a bit, and that's what I'd prefer to believe. Another explanation, however, has occurred to me. What if someone else once found themselves in this place I go to, and it made such an impression on him that when he got given the job of designing the Old Library, he based his design on what he'd once seen?)

The usual. I always know which scroll to pick, which is just as well, because although there's writing on the scroll-caps, it's in letters I can't read, though I do believe I've seen something similar before, on a worn old stone somewhere; anyhow, they're no help at all. I grab the scroll, undo the cap, tease out the parchment with thumbnail and forefinger; over to the chair, sit down; a boy falls out of an apple tree—ah yes, I remember it as though it were yesterday. There are dark clouds in the sky and I can smell the rain that's just about to fall. I tread on a windfall apple and it crunches under my foot. The cut on the boy's head is on the left side, about an inch long. I feel contempt, because he's crying. I roll up the parchment, and—

It does hurt the client, so I'm told. Not as bad as amputation or childbirth, but much worse than having a tooth pulled.

The old man had gone white, and was leaning back in his chair as though he'd been spread on it, like butter on bread. I ignored him. I turned to the young man and described the memory, slowly, in exact detail, stuff that wasn't in the old man's summary. His eyes opened very wide and he nodded.

You sure? I asked him. Quite sure, he said. That's just how I remember it.

I'd left out the contempt. I have my faults, but I'm not a bad person really.

I turned to the old man. He looked blank. I don't remember that at all, he said.

Indeed. Memory is such a slippery thing, don't you think? You think you remember something clear as daylight, but then it turns out you've been wrong all along; it was autumn, not winter, the horse was brown, not white, there were two men, not three, you heard the door slam after he came out, not before. Unreliable; but my unreliable memory is good enough to get you condemned to death in a court of law, provided I sound convincing and nobody spots the inconsistencies. And, furthermore, after a while memory is all there is—once a city stood here, or hereabouts; once there was a man called such-and-such who did these glorious or deplorable things; once your people slaughtered my people and drove them out of their own country. Only forget, and who's to say any of it ever happened? What's forgotten might as well never have existed.

Think of that. If there are no witnesses, did it really ever happen?

You know, of course. Even after the last witness has died, you still remember what you did.

That's why you need me.

———————

So I told them my terms of business. I remember the expression on the old man's face when I got specific about money. The young man gave him an oh-for-crying-out-loud look, and he pulled himself together. You must be a rich man by now, the old man said. I just grinned.

Right then, I said, tell me what you want.

The old man hesitated. Just a minute, he said. You can

take the memory out of someone's head, fine. So, do you remember it?

Of course, I told him. I just proved that.

Yes, he said, but afterwards. Does it stick or just fade away?

I kept my face straight. It sticks, I said. I have one of those special memories, I told him. Show me a page of figures, just a quick glance; five years later, I can recite it all perfectly. I remember everything.

He didn't like that one little bit. So I pay you to get rid of one witness, and in his place I get another one. With perfect recall. That's not a good deal.

I scowled at him. Total confidence, I said. I never tell. I'd rather die.

Sure, he said. You say that now. But what if someone gets hold of you and tortures you? They can make anybody talk, sooner or later.

I sighed. Oddly enough, I said, you're not the first person to think of that. Trust me, it's not a problem. It just isn't.

He was looking extremely unhappy, but I couldn't be bothered with all that. Take it or leave it, I said. That's how I do business. If you don't like it, don't hire me. I couldn't care less.

The young man leant across and whispered something in his ear. He whispered back. I could tell they were within an ace of getting really angry with each other. I made a big show of yawning.

The old man straightened his back and glowered at me. We'll trust you, he said. It's like this.

Believe me, I've heard it all, seen it all. I remember it all. Everything. If you can imagine it, I've got it tucked away in the back of my mind somewhere, vivid as if it were yesterday, sharp and clear as if I were standing there. Murder, rape, every kind of physical injury, every variation and subspecies of the malicious, the perverted, the degrading, the despicable; sometimes as victim, sometimes as perpetrator, surprisingly often as both. And, given the slippery nature of memory, does that mean I've actually suffered those things, *done* those things? Might as well have. Close enough, good enough. Do I wake up screaming at night? Well, no. Not since I learned how to distill poppies.

Turned out all they wanted me to fix was some trivial little fraud. There were two sets of accounts for the Temple charitable fund, and by mistake the younger man had let the auditor see the wrong ledger. No big deal. The auditor had told the old man, thirty per cent and I'll forget I ever saw anything.

I was relieved. The way they'd been carrying on, I expected a triple murder at the very least. I remembered to look grave and professional. I can handle that for you, I told them. But—

But?

I smiled. The price just went up, I said. And then I explained; as well as a really good memory, I'm blessed with an aptitude for mental arithmetic. If they were stewards of the White Temple charitable fund and they stood to save thirty per cent of their depredations through my intervention, the very least I could charge them was double the original estimate.

The old man looked shocked. So much dishonesty and bad faith in this world, his face seemed to say. That wasn't an estimate, he said, it was a fixed fee. You fixed it.

I grinned. It was an estimate, I said. Maybe your memory's playing tricks on you.

We haggled. In the end, we settled on three times the original estimate. When I haggle, I haggle rough.

They hadn't asked how I would go about doing it. They

never do.

Actually, it was a piece of cake. The auditor was a priest, and it's easy as pie to get a few moments alone with a priest. You go to confession.

"Bless me, Father," I said, "for I have sinned."

A moment's silence from the other side of the curtain. Then: "Go on," he said.

"I have things on my conscience," I said. "Terrible things."

"Tell me."

Oh, boy. Where to start? "Father," I said, "do we need to have this curtain? I don't feel right, talking to a bit of cloth."

I'd surprised him. "It's not a requirement," he said mildly. "In fact, it's there to make it easier for you to speak freely."

"I'd rather see who I'm talking to, if that's all right," I said.

So he pulled the curtain back. He had pale blue eyes. He was a nice old man.

I looked straight at him. "If I close my eyes," I said, "I can see it just as it happened."

"Tell me."

"If I tell you, will it go away?"

He shook his head. "But you'll know you've been forgiven," he said. "That's what counts."

So I told him, a round half-dozen memories. I think one of them was actually one of mine. He kept perfectly still. I think he'd forgotten to breathe. When I stopped talking, he said, "You did that?"

"I remember it as though it were yesterday."

"My son—" he said, and then words must have failed him. I could see he was suffering. I'm no angel, but I couldn't see any point in crucifying the old boy any further. I did the stare, and there I was inside his head, and it's never easy but these days it's nice and quick. I got what I came for, along with everything I'd just said to him, and then we were sitting opposite and he had this blank look on his face—

"Father?" I said.

He blinked twice. "My son," he said. I felt sorry for him. He'd just come round out of a daze, with no idea of who I was or why the curtain was drawn. "Well?" I said.

"Say six *sempiternas* and a *sacramentum in parvo*," he replied, without turning a hair. "And don't do it again."

I admire a professional. "Thank you, Father," I said, and left.

———————

My family and I never quite saw eye to eye. You know how it is. They had strong views about morality and duty and the reason why we're here; so did I, but they didn't coincide all that often. My family gradually came to the conclusion that they didn't like me very much. I can sympathise. As I think I've said, I'm no angel. Of course the faults weren't all on one side, they never are. But most of them were on mine. No point in denying that.

I remember how it all started. My sister and I were on our way back from town; we'd been sent to take five fleeces to the mill, but instead of hurrying straight back like we'd been told, we hung around until it was nearly dark. That meant we'd be late, a very serious crime, unless we took the forbidden short cut through Hanger copse—so naturally, that's what we did, and we made good time. We were through the thick of the wood and coming out into the fields. There was no path in Hanger, so there were places where you had to make your own way by pushing through. I ducked under this spindly little copper beech and bent a low branch out of the way; I remember telling myself, don't let go of the branch or it'll spring back and smack her in the eye. Then it occurred to me that letting go and smacking her in the face would be a good joke (I was, what, nine, ten years old) so I did just that. I didn't look round. I heard this terrible scream.

The stupid branch had hit her in the eye all right. It was all blood, welling up and pumping out of this impossible hole in her face. Then she covered it with her hands, still yelling. I realised what I'd done. I felt—well, you can imagine. Actually, no, you can't.

"Stop yelling," I said. "It's only a scratch. Here, let me look."

She shied away, like the calf you can't catch. "You did it on purpose."

"Don't be stupid."

"You did it on purpose. I know. I saw you."

I hate the truth sometimes. "I didn't," I said. "It was an accident. I'm sorry. It wasn't my fault."

You can't really lie to someone who knows the facts. She'd seen me; holding back the branch just long enough to giver her the impression it was safe to take the next step forward, then opening my hand, relaxing my grip, like an archer loosing an arrow, deliberate, precise, accurate. She'd witnessed it, she understood what I'd done, and she was going to tell on me.

I remember stooping down. There was this stone. You could kill someone with a stone like that.

"I can't see," she said. "You did it on purpose. You did."

I think I would have killed her, there and then. I was looking at her, I remember, not as my sister, a human being, but as a target—just there, I'd decided, above the ear; that's where the old man in the village got kicked by the horse, and he died just like that. I was staring at the exact spot; and then the side of her head seemed to melt away—

And that's a curious thing, because at that age I'd never seen a library, never even seen a book; heard of them, vaguely, like you've heard of elephants, but no idea what they looked like or how you used them. Goes without saying, I couldn't read. But I could; at least, I could read the books inside her head, well enough to find what I needed, the moment when I let go of the bent branch and it came swinging at her, filling her field of vision and blotting it out in red. I knew what to do, too. It came perfectly naturally, like milking a goat or killing a chicken. Like I'd been doing it all my life.

"Are you all right?" I said.

"My face hurts," she sobbed. "I can't see."

"What happened?"

"A branch jumped back and hit me in the eye."

"I'm sorry. I'm so sorry."

"Not your fault."

I remembered I was still holding the stone. I opened my fingers and let it drop. "It'll be all right," I remember telling her. "We'll get you home and then it'll all be just fine. You'll see."

It turned out that I was the hero of that story. They couldn't save the eye, of course. It was too far gone. But everyone said how well I'd handled the situation, how calm I was, how grown-up and sensible. And what the hell; why not? The bad thing had already happened, it was gone, past repair. If the truth had come out, it'd have torn our family apart, just think of all the damage it'd have done, to all of us, right down the line forever. There's too much unhappiness in the world as it is.

Anyhow, I think that was me. Pretty sure.

After all, what is truth but the consensus of memories of reliable witnesses? I think He (the fire-god, the Invincible Sun, whoever, whatever; I've had so many genuine mystical experiences, all totally convincing, most of them hopelessly contradictory) put me on this Earth as a sort of antidote to the truth—you know, like dock leaves and nettles. Under certain circumstances, I can do this amazing thing. I can reshape the past. I can erase truth. It sounds pretentious, but I regard it as my mission in life. Truth is like love; it's universally lauded and admired, and most of the time it just causes pain and makes trouble for people. Obviously, I can't be there for everybody, and there are some things so big and blatantly obvious that I can't do anything about them—the Second Social War, for example, or the Great Plague. But I stand for the wonderful revelation that the past is not immutable and the truth is not absolute. This ought to inspire people and give them hope. It doesn't, of course, because the essence of my work is that nobody knows about it, apart from the people who commission me (and half of them don't remember doing so, for obvious reasons), and they ain't telling.

The memory of a priest, however, is a real bitch. People confess to priests. I guess being a priest is the closest anybody normal ever gets to being me. They have to open their minds and their memories to all the poisonous waste of Mankind—imagine being a priest with a memory like mine, it'd kill you. They have their faith, of course, which is a wonderful thing. It must be like those gravel beds they build in watercourses, to filter out all the crap. Breaking into a priest's memory is, therefore, not something I enjoy.

Now I think I've given you the impression that I'm rather better at my job than I really am. I've let you think that I go in, get precisely what I want, and get out again, completely unaware of and unaffected by anything else that might be in there. If only. True, I only read—well, the titles of the scrolls, the list of contents, the index. That's bad enough. Each entry in the ledger (I'm beginning to realise how inadequate my library metaphor is; sorry) embodies a minuscule but intensely compressed summary. Your eye rests on it for a split second, and immediately you get the gist of it. I can skim down the average man's lifetime of memories in the time it takes you to read a page of your household accounts. But every entry is like a tiny, incredibly detailed picture, and I have (so to speak) exceptional eyesight.

Furthermore, some memories leak. They're so bright and sharp and vivid that they stand out, your eye's drawn to them, you can't help looking at them. I try and mind my own business, of course I do, but some things—

Like the men who murder their wives and the women who murder their children, the men who poison wells and kill whole towns, the rapists and the sadists and the broad rainbow spectrum of human maladjustment; and they go to their priests to get rid of it, and the priests take away the sins of the world and file them in their archives, and then I come along. I really don't like doing priests. It's like walking barefoot through a dark room with broken glass on the floor. Oh, and I did that once, or someone did. No fun at all.

———————

I went to where I was supposed to be meeting them. The young man was there; no sign of the old man. He was sitting on a bench in front of the Blue Star Temple, reading a book. He looked up as my shadow fell across the page.

"Well?" he said.

"All done."

He frowned at me, as though I were a spelling mistake. "How do I know that?"

I get tired sometimes. "You don't. Instead, you trust me and my colossal reputation among respected leaders of the community."

"You'll be wanting your money."

"Yes."

He moved his feet, and I saw a fat leather satchel. "You lunatic," I said. "I can't walk home carrying that. I wouldn't get a hundred yards."

"I got here just fine."

"You don't live where I do."

He shrugged. "Your problem," he said. "Well? Do you want to count it?"

I smiled at him. "People don't double-cross me," I said. "They simply wouldn't dare."

An unpleasant thought must have crossed his mind just then. "No, I don't suppose they would. Anyway, it's all there."

I leaned forward to take hold of the strap but he shifted his feet again. "We can trust you, can't we?"

"Of course."

"I mean," he went on, "we're not killers, my dad and I, or we'd have had that old fool's head bashed in. But there comes a point where you have to look beyond your principles, don't you know. I just thought I'd mention that."

I put the back of my hand against his calf and moved it sideways. Then I pulled the satchel out. It was reassuringly heavy. "Don't worry," I said. "I'm an honourable man."

"Really."

I stood up. I remember thinking; no, don't do it, there's no call for that sort of behaviour. "And I do try to give value for money," I said. "I want my customers to think they've got what they paid for. It's good for business."

"Right. Well, goodbye."

"So if I sense that a customer isn't satisfied," I went on, "I throw in something extra, for goodwill. He's not your father."

His eyes were very wide. "You what? What did you say?"

"Goodbye."

Actually, I was lying, though of course he had no way of knowing that. So what? He asked for it. The truly splendid, insidious thing about it is, when his father and mother eventually die and only he is left, the last surviving witness to those events, it *will be* true—in his mind, the only archive. So you see, I can create truth as well as delete it. Clever old me.

———————

Several of my clients, misguided souls who thought they wanted to get to know me better, have asked me how I got into this line of work in the first place. I tell them I can't remember.

There was this spot of trouble when I was seventeen. As I my have mentioned, I'm no angel. There was a small difficulty, and I had to leave home in rather a hurry. Luckily, it was a dark night and the people looking for me didn't know the countryside around our place as well as I did; their dogs were rubbish, too. I took the precaution of bringing along the clothes I'd been wearing the previous day and stuffing them inside a hollow tree I knew I'd be passing on the way out, so to speak. Fortuitously, it stood on the banks of the river. Stupid dogs all crowded round the tree, jumping up and yelling their heads off, while I swam upstream a bit, hopped out, and went on my way rejoicing. The men who were after me were livid, as you can imagine—I wasn't there to see, of course, but I remember the looks on their faces quite clearly. Gave me the best laugh I'd had in ages.

Still; once the warm inner glow of profound cleverness had worn off, I reflected on my position and found it largely unsatisfactory. There I was, sopping wet, one angel thirty to my name, no place to go, no friends, no identity. Naturally, I wasn't the first person in history to find himself in that state. After all, that's how cities came about in the first place; it's what they're for.

The nearest city was only twenty miles away. I knew it quite well, so it was useless; somebody would recognise me, and word would get about. My angel thirty would've been just enough to buy me a seat on the stage to the next city down the coast, but I decided not to risk it, since coachmen sometimes remember names and faces. As things had turned out, I'd left home in a pair of wooden-soled hemp slippers, the kind you wear for slopping about the house in. There wasn't much left of them by the time I dared risk stopping and thinking. They certainly weren't in a fit state to carry me eighty miles on bad roads, assuming I was prepared to take the chance of staying on the road, which I wasn't. Remember when you could buy a decent pair of boots for an angel thirty? You could back then; but first you have to find a shoemaker, for which you need a city. One damn thing after another.

I find that when you're in a deep pit of doubt and perplexity, Fate jumps in and provides you with an answer, almost invariably the wrong one. As in this case. First thing I saw when the sun rose was a farmhouse, practically rearing up on its hind legs at me out of the early morning mist. I thought; there'll be boots in there. I'll walk up to the door and offer to buy a pair. Easy as that.

Idiot. A stranger hobbling up out of nowhere wanting to buy footwear would tend to snag in the memory, particularly out in the wild, where nothing ever happens. I had good reason to wish not to be memorable. The hell with it, I thought. I was by now more or less resigned to the fact that I'm no angel; what's one more minor transgression? Be a man. Steal the stupid boots.

Sad fact. It's not enough to be a thief. You need to be a good thief. I'm not. My problem is, I don't look where I'm going. I try, ever so hard; but sooner or later there'll be a chair or a table or a tin plate or a bowl of apples that I somehow contrive to overlook. Crash it goes on the hard flagstone floor, and that's that. Here we go again.

The farmer was an old man, feeble, with a bad leg. I could've taken him easily. His son and his four grandsons were a different matter. What they were doing, hanging around the house when the sun was well up and they should've been out grafting, I have no idea. They didn't approve of thieves. There was an apple tree just outside the back door, with a low branch sticking out practically at a right angle. They had, they assured me, plenty of rope, not to mention a dung heap. And besides, they said, who'd miss me?

The human memory is a wonderful thing. They say that when you die, at the moment of departure, your entire life flashes past your eyes in a fraction of a second. This isn't actually true; but all sorts of stuff crowds into your mind when you're standing on the bed of a cart with a rope round your neck; among them, in my case, the circumstances of my sister's accident. To be honest, I hadn't given it much thought in the intervening time—tried to put it out of my mind, I guess, and who can blame me?— but it came right back to me at that precise moment, and I remember thinking, I wish I could do that trick where I went into her mind and pulled the memory out, it'd be really useful right now if I could do that. And suddenly I found I could.

False modesty aside, it was a tour de force. Six men and five women, one after the other, in a matter of seconds. I've done bigger jobs since, but that's with the benefit of considerable experience. For what was only my second go at it, I did remarkably well. Incentive helps, of course. It wasn't the neatest work I ever did, I had to hurt them quite a lot—like I cared—the pain kept them off balance and sort of woozy, which helped considerably. When I'd finished, we were left with this tableau; a kid standing on a cart under the apple tree, with six men and five women crowded round. No rope, I'd chucked that into the nettles. How we all got there, a total mystery to everybody except me.

I cleared my throat. I think my voice must've been a bit high and croaky, but I did my best. "Well, thanks for that," I remember saying. "I'd better be getting along."

One of the grandsons helped me down off the cart. He had a sort of dazed look. I took a long stride, and felt the dewy wet grass under my feet. "I almost forgot," I said. "The boots."

The old man looked at me. "What?"

"The boots," I repeated. "Really kind of you." He was still holding them in his hand; evidence, I guess. I reached out, took them, and pulled them on. Lousy fit, but what can you do? "Thanks again," I said, and walked quickly away. You learn not to look back. It takes some doing, but it's worth the effort.

———————

I'm not the sort of man that people tend to remember. Just look at me and you'll agree. I'm about five seven, thickset, small nose, small ears, low forehead, leg-of-pork forearms, the typical farm boy up from the country. I slip out of people's minds as easily as a wriggling fish. People hardly notice me, in the street, in a crowded room. Most of the time, I might as well not be there.

Remember what I told you about why I don't like doing priests? For three days afterwards, I wandered around feeling useless and stupid, like having a headache but without the pain. I knew there was something on my mind, but I couldn't figure out what it was. I filled the time in with chores. I bought a new (to me) pair of boots. I fixed the leak in the roof—at that time I was living in the roofspace above a grain store; one wall had cracked and was bulging out in a disturbing fashion, so it was empty until the owners raised the money to repair it; the rats had the ground floor, I had the penthouse. I mended both my shirts where they'd started to fray. Stuff like that.

And then, on my way to the market early, to see if I could buy some windfall apples cheap, I met a man I knew slightly. I pretended I hadn't seen him. He called out my name. I stopped.

"Long time no see," he said.

"I've been busy," I told him.

He nodded. "Working?"

"Yes."

"Splendid. Get paid?"

"Yes."

"In funds, then."

I sighed a little sigh. "Yes."

"Destiny," he said, and grinned. "Back of the Sincerity & Trust, one hour after sunset. Be there."

I walked away without saying a word.

I sometimes wonder if I'm like that hero in the old legends whose strength was as the strength of ten, but only as long as the sun was in the sky. In my case, strength of will. All that day, while the Invincible Sun rode the heavens, blessing us poor mortals with the sacrament of His light, I was utterly determined. I wasn't going. No force on Earth would get me within a mile of the Sincerity until noon tomorrow. Throughout the morning I felt the power within me grow; at midday, I was solid as a rock. I stayed that way till halfway through the afternoon, and as the shadows began to lengthen I kept checking up on myself, to see if my strength of purpose was going to hold out—and it did, right up till the first red streaks began to show in the sky. I don't know, maybe I'm more like a werewolf or something like that. Maybe it's the darkness that affects me, or more precisely the yellow glow of lighted windows. They call to me; come inside, they say, where it's warm and friendly. I noticed to my surprise that I was only two blocks from the Sincerity. The light was fading rapidly. I quickened my pace and walked the other way.

I believe it happens a lot in deserts. You walk and

walk and keep on walking, and suddenly you realise you've gone in a circle and you're back where you started from. In this case, just across the street from the back door of the Sincerity at one hour after sunset.

About half of them I knew, if only slightly. The usual crowd. They'd already started. A tall, thin elderly man I didn't know had the dice. He was trying to make six. A man I knew well tapped me on the shoulder, nodded, and said, "Bet?"

I shook my head. "Just here to watch."

He laughed. "Ten angels. I'll give you five to one."

"Bet."

The thin old man made his six. My ten angels had become fifty. I nearly always start off with a win.

So there I was, at dawn the next day, considerably poorer than the day I was born, but blessed with a useful skill with which I could earn money. Just as well, really.

I remembered that I had an appointment to see a prospective customer. I headed back home, washed, shaved, put on my clean shirt and my new boots. I'll say this for myself, I've got this gambling thing well under control now. As soon as I run out of money, I stop; I never ever play with markers or get into debt. Someone once told me I gamble so as to get rid of all the money I make. There may be something in that. If I'd kept what I've made over the years, right now I'd have more money than the government.

Disgustingly bright and early (I'm not a morning person) I walked out into Cornmarket, heading west. On the corner of Sheep Street and Coppergate I realised someone was following me. I didn't look round. I guess I'd detected him by the way his footsteps kept perfect time with my own—it sounds a bit paranoid, but I have experience in these matters, believe me. I did my best not to do anything that would let him know I'd noticed him.

I had two options. Either I could keep to the main streets, where there were plenty of people, or I could lead him off the beaten track down into the little dark alleys between Coppergate and Lower Town, where I stood a reasonable chance of losing him or jumping him. Like a fool, I chose the latter. In my defence, I would like to point out that I have the memories of God only knows how many fights, together comprising a better combat education that you'd get in any military academy anywhere. I know about that sort of thing.

Rather too much, in fact. Out back of the carpet warehouse in Tanners Yard there's an old gateway with two massive pillars; I'd noticed it a long time ago, with just such a contingency in mind. I led him there, ducked in between the pillars, and vanished. He stopped and looked round to see where I'd gone. As soon as his back was turned, I was on him like the proverbial snake.

The law in these parts disapproves of carrying weapons of any sort in public places, but since when is three feet of waxed string a weapon? Answer; when you slip it over a man's head, cross the ends over at the base of his neck, and pull hard. My trouble is, I don't know my own strength.

I was so stunned and disgusted with myself that I was almost too late to get inside his head before all the lights went out. It was a scramble. I know from experience, it's not pleasant to be in there when someone dies. I had just enough time to grab what I wanted and run.

Sure enough (I stood over him, looking down); he'd been hired by one of my satisfied customers, for five angels. I ask you, five angels. It's about time the hired killers in this town got organised.

───────

Well, it's inevitable. When I consume the memory of the last surviving witness, I become the last surviving witness, and there's nobody to clear out my head cleanly and humanely. You can't blame them; I don't. My set scale of fees includes a levy, to cover the inconvenience and mental trauma of monotonously regular attempts on my life.

But I don't hold it against my clients. I can't afford to.

When you've been inside someone's head, you know him, intimately; what he looks like is substantially irrelevant and uninteresting. I turned him over with my foot. Age thirty-five (I already knew that), the big, hollow frame of an ex-soldier who hasn't been eating too well lately. He had red hair and blue eyes. So what?

I always reckon that you gain something from pretty well every experience, however bad it may be. From him (whoever he was) I took away a picture of dawn in the Claygess Mountains, a rapturous explosion of light, blue skies, green fir trees, and snow. Just thinking of it makes me feel clean. That and a move whereby, when someone's behind you and strangling you, a slight rearrangement of the feet and shift of your centre of balance enables you to throw them over your shoulder like a sack of feathers. If he'd remembered it a trifle earlier, he'd probably have made it. Ah, well.

By a curious coincidence, the man who'd hired him to kill me was the man I was on my way to meet. He was surprised to see me.

"You said you had a job for me," I said.

"Changed my mind."

"Ah." I nodded slowly. "In that case, there's just the matter of my consultancy fee."

He looked at me. Sometimes I think I'm not the only one who can see inside people's heads. "Fine," he said. "How much?"

"Five hundred angels."

He licked his lips. "Five hundred."

"Yes."

"Draft? On the Gorgai brothers? I haven't got that much in cash."

I know the Gorgai brothers better than they know themselves. "All right," I said.

I stood over him while he wrote, then thanked him politely and left. I felt happy; I was back in the money again. Happiness in this world is by definition a transitory state, and two small tumbling ivory cubes put me back where I'd started from twelve hours later, but at least I had the memory of being rich, for a little while. Only memory endures. I learned that the hard way.

———

Two days later I had another client, a genuine one who paid. It was a something-and-nothing job, really rather touching; he was fifty-six and rich and wanted to marry again, but there was this one memory of his dead wife that really broke him up, and could I help? Of course. To me, it was just an image of a moderately pretty girl in old-fashioned clothes arranging flowers, in a bay window in an old house in the country. When I'd finished he gave me that blank look; *I know who you are and why you're here, but I have no idea why it was so important.* It sort of offends me that when I do my best work, the customer hasn't a clue how much I've done for him. It's like painting a masterpiece for a blind patron.

———————

I distinctly remember the next time I met the old man and his son.

I was fast asleep, and then I hit the floor and woke up. The last time I fell out of bed, I was four (I remember it well).

I opened my eyes, and saw a ring of faces looking down at me. Two of them I recognised. The old man said, "Get him up."

Two of the other faces grabbed my arms and hauled me upright. They were strong and not very gentle. I know half a dozen ways of dealing with a situation like that, but those memories came from men twice my weight, and besides, I wasn't in the mood.

"You betrayed us," the old man said.

I was stunned. "Me? God, no, I'd never do a thing like that. Never."

For that I got a fist like oak in my solar plexus. "Who did you tell?" the old man asked. Stupid; I couldn't answer, because I had no breath in my body. "Who did you tell?" the old man repeated. I tried to breathe in, but I was all blocked up inside. I saw him nod, and someone hit me again. "What did you do with the money you stole from us?" I shook my head. "I never stole from you, I wouldn't dare." Then someone threw a rope over the crossbeam of the rafters directly overhead. *Oh,* I thought.

"One more time," the old man said. "Who did you tell?"

I couldn't speak, so I mouthed the word; *nobody.* Someone behind me dropped the noose over my head. "Get on with it," the old man said. I tried to think of something to say, a lie, something he'd want to hear, but—here's an interesting fact for you. When you're winded so bad you can't breathe, you can't lie, your imagination simply blanks out and making stuff up is impossible, you just can't do it. You don't have the strength, simple as that.

Someone hauled on the rope. I felt my feet lift off the ground. I felt this excruciating pain. And then—

———————

But I'm getting ahead of myself.

This clerk came to see me; a boy, seventeen at most, with a long turkey neck and big ears. He worked for them, the old man and his son. They were pleased with the job I'd done for them, and would I help them out with another little problem? You'll recall that I was broke again at this point. Depends what it is, I replied. The clerk said he didn't know the details, but to meet them outside the Flawless Diamonds of Orthodoxy at third watch that evening. What about the curfew? I asked. The boy just grinned nervously and gave me a piece of paper. It was a draft on the Merchant Union, two hundred angels.

"He betrayed us," the old man told me. It was dark and bitter cold, and I'd come out without my scarf (now I come to think of it, I'd traded my scarf for a loaf of bread). "He'll deny it, of course. He'd rather die than tell. That's what we need you for."

The rest you know. They picked the lock and we all trooped up the stairs quiet as little mice; they woke him up by pulling him out of bed onto the floor. He claimed he was innocent and hadn't betrayed them or stolen from them, not a bent stuiver. After a while, they threw a rope over a rafter and hung him. I was inside his mind when he died. He'd been telling the truth. He was a lawyer, by the way, acting for the Temple oversight committee.

"Well?" the old man asked me.

"Nothing," I told him. "He was telling the truth. He didn't betray you. He didn't steal anything." I paused. "I could've told you that anyhow. There was no need—"

I got frowned at for that, so I shut up. Customers always think they know best. "You sure?"

"Positive," I said. "If he'd had that on his mind, I'd have seen it. But there wasn't anything."

I got the feeling he didn't believe me. Stupid. Why would I lie? Well, obviously, if I meant to blackmail them or sell them out to their enemies; but I wouldn't do that, because it'd be unprofessional. I may be no angel but I have standards. Of course, they had no way of knowing that.

"Get out," the old man said. "And keep yourself available. We may want you again."

"You've just made me accessory to a murder," I said. "I'm not pleased about that."

He shook his head. "Not murder," he said. "Suicide. And don't you ever talk back to me. Got that?"

I considered the evidence of my own eyes. There's this man, hanging from a rafter. The only chair in the room is lying on its side, right under his dangling feet. No sign of forced entry, or anyway, there won't be, ten minutes from now. Sure looks like suicide, and the only evidence to the contrary is a memory. "Point taken," I said. It's amazing how many people construe that as *yes*. "Suicide," I said. "Silly me. I'll go now."

"Hold on." The younger man was looking at me. "Before he goes, he can make himself useful."

The old man looked at him; he was nodding stupidly at the hired men. Oh, come on, I thought, there's six of them. "That's a point," the old man said.

"You can't afford it," I told him.

He grinned at me. "Reduced rate for quantity. Or you could be feeling really depressed and sad."

Oh, I thought. Sad enough to jump off the Haymarket bridge, and (as the man said) who would miss me? Fair enough. "Tell you what," I said. "This one's on the house."

The young man grinned. The old man said he wouldn't hear of it. The labourer is worthy of his hire. So I did all six of them for fifteen angels each.

Not that it mattered all that much. Forty-eight hours later I was broke again.

The point being; I died in that room. I know I did, because I remember it clear as day.

I died, but here I am. Explain that, if you can. Simple. I died, and I was born again, just like it says in the Testament. Proof positive. I have difficulty with the faith aspect of it, but the plain facts admit of no other explanation. Blessed are those who have seen and yet have believed.

———————

We call them the Temple trustees and everybody knows who we mean, but their proper name is the Guardians of the Perpetual Fund for the Proliferation of Orthodoxy. They're serious men, and they own all the best grazing land from the Hog's Back right out to the Blackwater, as well as half the prime real estate in the Capital and a whole lot of other nice things, all of which came into the possession of the Fund through the bequests and endowments of former Guardians. The income from these assets is divided between the Commissioners of the Fabric, who maintain and improve the Temple buildings throughout the empire, and the Social Fund, which pays for the soup kitchens and the way stations and the diocesan free schools, not to mention the travelling doctors and the Last Chance advocates who defend prisoners on capital charges who haven't got the money to hire a real lawyer. I seem to remember someone telling me that about a third of the wealth of the empire passes through the trustees' hands, and that the trustees themselves are chosen from the select few who have the brains to do the job and so much money of their own that they have no possible incentive to steal; in fact, you have to pay an annual fee equivalent to the cost of outfitting and maintaining a regiment in the field in order to belong to the College of Guardians, and there's a waiting list a mile long. It's probably quite true. When you're that rich, money is just a way of keeping score.

That was the sort of people I was dealing with; rich, powerful men, peers of the gods, the sort who make and alter truth—What is truth? Truth is what you know, if you're one of them. Truth is what you own. If the whim takes you, you can say, "On the banks of the Blackwater there's a city constructed entirely of marble." Actually, no, there isn't. "Oh, yes, there is. I had it built, last week." Or: "There never was a war between the Blemyans and the Aram Chantat." You go to the Temple library to look up the references to refute this idiotic statement, and all the relevant books are missing all the relevant pages. Or: "Who? There's no such person." Indeed. Men like gods who can ordain the future, regulate the present, and amend the past—pretty well everything worthwhile that ever happened in history was done by men like that; they built cities, instituted trade and manufacture, fostered the sciences and the arts, and endowed charities. *Let it be so,* they said, and it was so. And, quite rightly, what they paid for, they own: the freeholds, the equity. And us. Without them, we'd be dressed in animal skins and living in caves. I believe in them, the way I believe in the Invincible Sun—which is to say, I acknowledge their existence, and their authority, and their power. Doesn't mean I have to like them. Or Him, for that matter.

———————

When I was nineteen, not long after I left home, I met this girl. I can close my eyes and picture her exactly, as though Euxis the Mannerist had painted her on the inside of my eyelids. Not that Euxis would've accepted the commission, since he only ever painted incarnations of perfection, absolute physical beauty—and she was hardly that. Pretty, yes, but—my mother had a saying, *she's prettier than she looks.* And anyway, Euxis wasn't all that good. He couldn't do hands worth spit.

The good thing about the way she looked was that she inspired no interest in the handsome, rich, charming young men who could've taken her away from me just by noticing her. Don't get me wrong, she wasn't that sort of girl, but I know perfectly well that some things are outside one's control. Beauty, of course, is one of them.

Alongside the rich, in the pantheon of gods, are the beautiful. They too can change the world, a smile here, a frown there. They can inspire and kill love as easily as a rich man can endow a hospital or arrange a murder, and they do it because they can. But I worshipped her because she was no goddess, and if only there were someone else who could do what I can do, I'd pay him anything he asked for to get her out of my mind. She died, you see, and when I went down on my knees and prayed to the gods to bring her back to life, they just ignored me. Forget her, they told me, move on. I can only assume they were trying to be funny. Anyhow, I won't forget that in a hurry, believe me.

My next job for the old man and his son was quick, easy, and safe, or so they told me. A business associate of theirs was to be entrusted with certain sensitive information in order to carry out a certain confidential transaction on their behalf. Once the deal had been done, I was to remove the whole episode from his memory. He had (they told me) been fully informed about my special abilities, and had readily agreed to the procedure. He would just sit there, perfectly still and quiet, while I did my thing. In spite of this, I would be paid the same fee I'd received for more arduous work.

At the time I was not well off for money, as a result of some unsatisfactory experiments into certain aspects of probability theory. One of the worst things about poverty is that when people like the old man call on you, you're actually glad to see them. Delighted, I told them, and thank you for your valued custom. They told me a time and a place. I promised I'd be there, and went away to wash my other shirt, because a smart appearance creates a good impression.

If they're worth the money, you don't notice them, not until they're right on top of you and there's nothing you can do. These two—I wish I knew their names, so that I could hire them myself if I ever need any help with violence. One of them was vaguely familiar, I may have caught a glimpse of him in the street at some point over the last few days (I never forget a face) and thought nothing of it; the other one I'd never seen before in my life. They hit me with a short wooden club and dropped a sack over my head, and that was that.

When the sack came off, I barely noticed, because the room was dark. I was vaguely aware of the shape of a man not far away. I was sitting down, but my hands and feet were tied. I heard a man's voice, not the man whose shape I could just make out. It said, "This thing you do."

I waited. Someone nudged the back of my head with

a sharp object. "Yes?" I said.

"The person you do it to," the voice went on. "Do they know about it?"

"It hurts," I replied. "But they don't necessarily realise it's me doing it. They may think it's a heart attack, or something like that."

"So it hurts a lot."

"Yes."

Pause for mature consideration. Then I screamed, because someone was holding a red-hot iron to the back of my neck. "As bad as that?"

It took me a moment to catch my breath. "Different sort of pain, I think," I said. "But purely in terms of quantity, about that, yes."

"Mphm." I heard movement behind me, and the cherry-red end of an iron rod appeared in front of my eyes. "Can you make it a bit less painful, if you really try hard?"

"No," I said. From a slight intake of breath, I guessed I'd said the wrong thing. "Of course, I can remove the memory of the pain. That's easy."

(A slight overstatement; like saying the sea is a bit damp. But I can do that, yes.)

"Ah." He liked me again. The red-hot iron went away, though probably only as far as a charcoal brazier. "So you can do it to someone and he won't know about it."

53

"Yes."

"Splendid." Slight pause. "Now, I'm going to ask you that again, and this time, if you were lying, tell the truth. You can do it to someone and he won't know?"

"Yes. You have my word."

I'd said something funny. "Fair enough," said the voice. "The word of a gentleman is always good enough for me. Now, then. You work for—" And he mentioned two names. They weren't the names I knew the old man and his son by, but I'd done a little research. "Yes," I said, and braced myself for another touch of the hot iron.

"Relax," the voice said. "I'm not going to ask you to betray confidences, I know you wouldn't do that." Pause. "Not for some time, and by then you'd be no good for anything. But I am going to ask you to do something that isn't in the best interests of your employers. I'm going to ask you to bleach something out of their minds. Would that be awkward for you, ethically speaking?"

Believe it or not, I did actually think about it before answering. Not for terribly long. "No," I said, "that wouldn't be a problem." Silence; so I expanded a little. "My duty to my client is not to divulge things he doesn't want known. That's it, as far as I'm concerned."

"Particularly if he never knows about it."

"Particularly, yes."

The voice laughed gently. "Because if nobody knows

about it, it never happened. Splendid. I believe your usual charge is a thousand angels."

Wonderful, what people believe. But I have nothing against good honest faith. We could do with more of it in this world. "That's right, yes."

"Two thousand angels, since there are two of them, father and son."

I was beginning to warm to him. "That's right, yes."

"The rest of you, out." Shuffling noises. The man in front of me stood up and walked away. A door closed. "Now I'm going to tell you what I need you to remove. I know I can trust your discretion, because you're a gentleman. Listen carefully."

———

Burns on the back of the neck are no fun at all; every time you turn your head, you stretch them, and it hurts. Something to remember him by.

Still; two thousand angels. I lay awake (on my face; I can only get to sleep lying on my side) all that night thinking of what I could do with two thousand angels. Buy a large farm, fully stocked, and hire a good bailiff. Or invest in shipping, which is going to be the next big thing, or copper mines in Scheria (or maybe not; too much of a gamble for my taste). Give up work for good. Get rich.

Become a god.

Two days to go before I next saw the old man and his son; in the meanwhile, I had a piffling little job to get out of the way. Two hundred angels practically for nothing.

He was an inoffensive old boy, well into his eighties, living in a smart house overlooking the bay—he'd been a ship's captain, and he liked to see the sails in the harbour. His servant brought me green tea in a little porcelain bowl, and some wafer-thin biscuits that tasted of honey and cinnamon. I sat on a big carved rosewood chair made for someone twice my size. It was all very civilized.

He told me about his son; a good boy, very clever, took after his mother. My client had just bought his own ship, after a lifetime of hard work and being careful with money. Naturally, he wanted his son to come and work with him, but the boy had set his heart on being a musician. He could play the flute very well (but all technique and no feeling). It was what his mother would have wanted, he kept on saying. My client was heartbroken, because the whole idea of the ship was so he could pass it on to his son and heir. There were harsh words, and the boy slammed out of the house. He got a job playing the flute in a teahouse down by the docks; and there he died, on account of slow reflexes when the furniture started to fly. I think about him every day, the old man said, and it's killing me.

Well, I thought, what do you expect? Serves you right for meddling with love. You'll get no sympathy from me. But he'd been very polite and given me a nice cup of tea, and two hundred angels was two hundred angels more than I had in the world, and I am, after all, a professional. "How can I help?" I asked.

"I want to forget him," he said. "I want to forget he was ever born."

I got up. I think I said thank you for the tea. I told him, sorry, I can't help you, I'm really sorry and I wish there was something I can do, but I can't. He accepted it quietly, like the prisoner who's pleaded guilty. Because he was such a nice old fellow, I tried really hard to keep the loathing off my face, at least until the door closed behind me.

(Sometimes I wonder, what if none of this is really me? What if—for an obscene amount of money—I was at some point hired to take over someone's entire life, from birth, every memory, the lot; and what if every memory I think is mine is really that other man's, a complete and coherent narrative, utterly vivid and real in my head, perfect and irrefutably valid, subject to corroboration and proof from external sources, except that it actually happened to somebody else? I guess it's one of those fantasies you spin to keep yourself going; like, my parents aren't really my parents, really I'm the son of a duke, stolen from his cot by tinkers, and one day my real father will turn up and claim me, and take me back to my real life, the one I should have had all along?)

———

On my way to meet the old man and his son, I ran into someone I knew.

By the time I saw him, it was too late for evasive action. I looked round to see if there was anyone to hear if I yelled for help—no such luck; I was taking my usual shortcut through the Caulkers' Yards. Maximum privacy. Serves me right for being too lazy to walk down Crowngate.

He smiled at me. "Been looking for you," he said.

Too big to fight, too nimble to evade. "I've got your money," I said.

"No," he said. "You haven't."

"I'll have it for you by tonight, that's a promise."

"Two angels sixteen," he said. "I want it now."

"Be reasonable," I started to say, but then he kicked me in the groin and I fell down. I twisted as I went down and landed on my shoulder, absorbing most of the impact in muscle. After a while, it becomes second nature.

"But it's all right," he said, and kicked me in the ribs. "I'm patient, I can wait." Another kick. His heart wasn't in it, though, I could tell. "Here, tonight, fourth watch. Three angels."

Of course. Interest on two angels sixteen. He's not very good at basic arithmetic, but he doesn't need to be. "No problem," I whispered. "I'll be here."

"You'd better be." He gave me a look of infinite contempt. "It's so easy for you rich bastards, never had to do a day's work in your lives. Plenty more where that came from. You think you're so much better. You make me sick." A third kick, for luck; this time with feeling. "And don't ever borrow money from me again."

I waited till he'd gone, and picked myself up slowly. It took a while. To be fair to myself, I'd only borrowed from him because he'd just won everything I had, well, everything I had left. Over the years he's had enough money out of me to pay the revenues for Moesia province, including the charcoal levy. But he dresses like trash and lives in a coal cellar. Beats me what he spends it all on.

Fortunately he'd done no irreparable visible damage. I dusted myself off and limped the rest of the way as quickly as I could manage. I'm proud to say I was on time for my appointment, in spite of everything.

———————

My victim was a fine-looking man, about forty years old, tall and broad-shouldered, with a farmer's tan. He was reclining on a couch, with a silver goblet at his elbow and a plate of those minced-up fish nibbles in wafer-thin crispy pastry shells. He didn't stand up when I entered the room, but there was a sort of involuntary movement which told me he'd considered it before deciding it wouldn't be appropriate.

The young man was wearing one of those fashionable silk robes; it was far too big for him and, in a moment of inspiration, I realised it was one of his father's hand-me-downs. The old man was wearing quilted wool (in summer, dear God) with frayed cuffs and elbows. The rich, bless them.

"This is the man I was telling you about," the old man said. "It won't take two minutes, and it doesn't hurt."

My victim frowned beautifully. "And he won't remember anything?"

I cleared my throat, but the old man answered for me. "He remembers all right," he said, "but he won't say anything. And besides, look at him. Who'd believe him?"

Uncalled for; I was wearing my good shirt, which fortunately hadn't come to harm to anything like the same extent as I had. "I take my clients' confidences very seriously," I said. I don't think anybody heard me.

"Up to you," my victim said. "It's your risk, after all."

The young man pulled a miserable face, which got him a scowl from his father. "We might as well get on with it," the old man said.

My victim shrugged. "What do I do?"

"Nothing," the old man said. "Just sit there."

I knew exactly what to look for, so it was a nice, easy job, in and out; I confess, my mind wasn't really on it, preoccupied as I was with the job I had to do on the old man and his son immediately afterwards, which would be much harder. I remembered to wipe the memory of the pain I'd caused him—he actually yelled out loud, with his eyes shut—and then straight on to do the old man and his son, while he was recovering from the shock.

By now you should have a pretty good idea of how I operate, so I won't bore you with a blow-by-blow; we can get a bit ahead of ourselves, to the point where I was shown out into the street (not the same one I'd come in by; the servants' entrance opened onto the stable yard, which led to a long mews, which opened into a winding high-walled alley that led eventually to Haymarket). I was in a pretty good mood. I'd done a pretty spectacularly impressive job on the old man and his son, professionally speaking, one of the highlights of my career so far—if my profession had learned journals and more than one practitioner, I could have written it up in a paper and been invited to speak at seminars. I'd got out of there in one piece. And I had money. I had a draft on the Diocesan Loan from the old man, and an escrow note from my other customer which I was now clear to cash in; a vast amount of money, enough for a new beginning, a clean slate, the wherewithal to be born again, washed in the blood of the Invincible Sun. It made me smile to think I'd been beaten up only an hour earlier for a tenth of one per cent of what I now possessed. If there'd been a puddle in the alley, I'd have walked on its surface without wetting my boots.

It was bleachingly hot in Haymarket, with the sunlight reflected off the broad white marble frontages. I walked up as far as the Stooping Victory, turned left into Palace Yard, called in at the Diocesan Loan, who settled my note without giving any indication that I was visible. Then down the steps opposite the Mercury Fountain to the Stamnite Brotherhood, who confirmed that the escrow on my note had been lifted and paid me out in twenty-angel pieces, fresh from the Mint, the edges of the flans still slightly sharp. Two doors down from the Stamnites is the Social and Benificent Order, the only bank in the Capital I'd trust as far as I could sneeze them. I paid in the lot, less five angels. And if I write a note on any of it in the next ten days, I told them, don't honour it, tear it up. Yes, sir, as though I'd made a perfectly reasonable request. Not their place to understand, just to do as they're told; the proper attitude of acolytes towards gods, after all.

(Bear in mind what I told you earlier, about my amazing strength of mind. The point being, it was just before noon by this stage, when the Sun is nearing His highest point, and my strength was therefore as the strength of ten. Where I usually go wrong is getting paid in the evening.)

The rest of the day—the rest of my life—was my own. I wandered down to the Old Market, sat at a table under a plane tree outside one of those high-class teashops and ordered green tea and a honeycake. I needed to sit down; the implications of what I'd just done—the proper word, actually, would be "achieved"—were only just starting to percolate through. I'd been paid for a big job, got my hands on enough money, and instead of rushing out and gambling the lot away as quickly as I could, I'd put it away safe in a bank, with measures in place to stop me getting at it. I'd done it quickly and without thinking, the way an experienced killer does a murder. That's the key, where irrevocable actions are concerned. Don't stop to think about it until it's done and too late.

They brought me my tea. When I tried to pay, they looked at me; sorry, we don't have change for a five-angel. I remembered I was a god. Send someone to the money-changers, I said. It's fine, I'm not in a hurry.

While I was waiting for my change, I tried hard to think seriously about the morning's momentous events. But I couldn't; not deliberately, like that. Instead, my mind skidded off and started to wander, and I thought about the good-looking man, my willing victim. Now here's a thing about what I do. I don't peek. Really. Why the hell should I want to take on more memories than I have to? But it's a bit like lawyers. Apparently, when they enter a room where there are documents, they automatically read them, quickly, at a glance, upside down even; it's second nature, they can't help it, and it's amazing how much they can read of a document just by looking at it. Same, I think, with me. I don't deliberately browse the other memories. I just glance, while looking for the one I'm after. But even a glance takes in a lot. Like those freaks or geniuses or whatever (actually, I'm one of them) who can see a painting, say, for a fraction of a second out of the corner of their eyes, and a week later describe the whole scene to you in precise detail.

The point being, as I sat in my shady seat drinking my delicious tea, I could recall with total clarity some of the glimpses I'd taken of the good-looking man's memory. It was probably because I was in a hurry and preoccupied; I hadn't made a conscious effort not to. The closest thing—I'm no great shakes at explaining, you can tell—would be getting through brambles. If you're patient and careful, you pick your way, carefully lifting the flailing tendrils out of the way, tenderly disengaging the ones that hook into you, and you come out unscathed. If you just bustle through, you get scratched to hell and your coat's covered in leaves and bits of briar.

There was a memory that just seemed to leap out and flood my mind. I was a soldier, and I was in a trench. I could smell the clay, which was wet and sticky underfoot. We were trying to climb out of the trench, but the sides were too steep and the clay was too hard to get a toehold in. I was shouting, because I was the officer and we were supposed to be attacking; I really didn't want anything to do with it, because I was terrified and worn out, and as far as I could see the job was impossible; but I was yelling, Come on, you bone-idle, chickenshit sons of bitches (and my fingers were clawing at the clay, but I couldn't get a grip); the men were scrambling, jumping—frantic, as if my shouting were wild dogs snapping at their legs, as if they were desperately trying to run away, not charge into battle; and the more they tried, the more I had to try too. I remember I got my left foot braced on a small chunk of stone sticking out of the trench wall; I put my weight on it and boosted myself up, clawed for a handhold, couldn't find one; my foot was slipping off the stone, which was tapered, not the right shape; it came off like a cam completing its stroke, and I slithered three feet down the trench wall, with my face in the clay, there was blood in my mouth and my lower lip was hard as a rock, I was sure I must've ripped my nose and chin off. I landed on my right ankle, badly; felt it turn over under my full weight, and something gave, and it hurt so much I screamed. I tried to stand up, but my leg just folded; and someone behind me used my head as a stepping-stone—the hobnails on his soles getting traction on my scalp—and flung himself at the lip of the trench; I saw him hanging by his fingertips, dragging himself up until his chin was over the top; and then he dropped back, a dead weight, and landed on my outstretched leg, and there was a crack as the bone broke; and there was an arrow in his forehead, clean through the bone, just above the left eyebrow.

I must've passed out at that point, because the memory ended abruptly. Thank you so much for that, I thought. Just what I needed.

Describing it like I've just done makes it sound like I lived through it all, half an hour or a quarter of an hour or however long it took. Not so. All over and done with in the time it takes to touch a tea-bowl to your lower lip. I put down the bowl and frowned. Sudden unsolicited episodes of memory aren't exactly uncommon—well, you do it all the time, don't you?—and I've learned to take them in my stride, as far as that's possible. But there was something else about that one, quite apart from its rather grisly subject matter. The grisliness was neither here nor there. I've got far worse stuff than that stowed away in my head. Rather, it was a sort of familiarity—no, wrong word, hopelessly wrong, giving you entirely the wrong idea, I'm so useless with language. All my memories are familiar, of course they are. You know that thing they call déjà vu? Like that, always. But this one—it's like that time (can't remember if it was me or someone else) when I walked into the house of someone I'd never met before, and there on the table was a candlestick, and I was absolutely certain I'd seen it before. I picked it up (my host gave me a funny look, but I didn't care) and examined it, looking for details of decoration and design; I very nearly said to him, you bastard, you stole my candlestick. But before I did that, I remembered that the one I had back home, sitting on the upturned water barrel that serves me as a table, was one of a pair; the one I was looking at was my candlestick's twin, hence the familiarity.

Like that—

I drank my tea. To push the analogy where it was reluctant to go, it felt like I'd managed to acquire the twin memory of one I already had—but it doesn't work like that, does it? And besides, I have perfect recall, and I couldn't remember another episode in a clay trench in the war. I was absolutely certain I'd never broken my leg; that's not the sort of thing you forget, even if you're capable of forgetting—

(I assume I'm incapable of forgetting, because I've never been aware of having done so. Exactly. Circular argument.)

The honeycake wasn't bad, though I wish they wouldn't overdo it by piling on the cinnamon. The man came back with my change. I left a two-stuiver tip. You can afford to be generous when you've got more money than God.

———

A hero like me (my weakness is heroic; it's a recurring theme in the mythologies of most cultures) fears nothing but fear itself; I'm shit-scared of fear, the very thought of it makes me go all to pieces. As the sun went down, I had this overwhelming urge to barricade myself in my loft, chain myself to the rafters, anything to keep from going out into the gathering darkness to where the dice fall and the cards are dealt. But I'd given my word of honour, so I had to go. If you can't trust a god, who can you trust?

Don't answer that.

I stopped off at a certain low-profile all-night dealership on the way, but I was still early; he didn't turn up until well after curfew. I stepped out from behind a pillar, and he didn't see me until it was too late.

I drew my sword and hit him between the shoulder blades with the pommel-nut. I recommend this move; you knock all the air out of a man's body without causing permanent damage. He's helpless, you can do what you like. I grabbed him and turned him round, then brought the pommel-nut down as hard as I could on his collarbone. It's one of the most painful things you can do to anybody. His mouth opened, and no sound came out. I stepped back to half measure and touched the point of the blade to his neck. "I've brought you your money," I said.

He was staring at me. He made me feel like I was unimaginably horrifying, the sort of thing you can't see without losing your mind. I liked that. I gave him a little prod with the sword, almost enough to draw blood but not quite. "Three angels," I said. "Hold out your hand."

He couldn't. He was too numb from the pain. So I came forward, grabbed his hand, pulled it toward me, and opened the balled fingers. Tucked inside my palm were the coins. I released them into his hand and closed his fingers around them.

"Pleasure doing business with you," I said.

The plan was to kick him in the nuts, to keep him busy while I withdrew, but there was no need. I slid the sword back into its scabbard under my coat, turned, and walked away. After I'd gone a few yards I turned and looked. He was still standing there, frozen. Not sensible, to stay perfectly still for any length of time in that neighbourhood, if you've got money on your person. But so what? Am I my brother's keeper?

———————

How do you suppose you'd feel if, after many trials and tribulations and having endured many sorrows along the way, you arrived at the satisfactory culmination of your adventures, with every loose end tied off and all outstanding issues dealt with finally and symmetrically? As though your life were a perfectly told story, concluded with a magnificent flourish?

I went home, pausing only to dump the sword down a well (not the sort of thing you'd want to be caught with on the streets at night, even if you're a god). I re-alised I was starving hungry, but there was nothing to eat apart from a stale quarter-loaf and a sliver of cheese rind. Forget it, I told myself; tomorrow you'll be out of here forever. Then I remembered I couldn't touch my money for another ten days—ah, well. That gave me ten days to select a gentleman's residence and deal with the legal formalities; in the meantime, I still had a whole angel, enough to buy plenty of good, wholesome food for a fortnight. I was very nearly out of lamp oil, so I snuffed the lamp and sat there in the dark most of the night, waiting to be reborn.

I think I fell asleep just before dawn, because when the knock on the door woke me up, I was groggy and stupid, and the light through the hole in the roof was very early morning, by its tone and angle. I got up off the floor and staggered to answer the door.

There was this woman. She looked at me, but didn't say what she was thinking. Instead, she said, "Excuse me, but are you the man who takes away memories?"

She was probably about forty-five, or a bit older; not younger. She had a thin face, and clothes that had cost a fair bit of money a long time ago. Someone had put in a lot of time and effort keeping them neat and clean over the years. "Yes," I said, "but I'm retired now. Sorry."

"It's my daughter," she said. "It's so bad, and I don't know what to do."

I looked at her. I can't read minds, but I've been in business a long time, so I can guess. "You'd better come in," I said.

"I haven't got much money."

"No," I said, "I don't suppose you have."

I was right. Three days earlier, her daughter had been raped by three men on her way back from Temple. Since then she hadn't said a word, hadn't eaten anything, just sat and stared at something nobody else could see. Her mother had six angels, but she was sure she could borrow another six. She was terribly afraid her daughter was going to die.

I looked at her. "Do I know you?" I said.

She shrugged. "I don't think so."

"Don't worry about it," I said. "I have this terrible memory."

She didn't try to answer that. "Will you help her?" she said. "Please?"

The bad thing about being a god is that people pray to you. I said nothing. I think that hurt her more than a sharp blow to the collarbone. I'm no angel, but I do feel things. "If it's the money," she said, "I can go to a moneylender or something. Please?"

I sighed, and I remember thinking, maybe this is how it is for the Invincible Sun, who takes away the sins of the world. Easy, glib phrase, that—you say it twice a day at Offices, but have you stopped to think what it actually means? I have. The idea is He takes your sins, the loathsome and unbearable things you've done, and he *transfers them to Himself*; it's as if He'd done them, not you, for all practical purposes He *has* done them, and all the guilt and pain and self-disgust are His now, not yours, and you're free and clear. Just imagine how much love and goodness it'd take to make anyone do a thing like that.

Still; I don't suppose He *enjoys* it; and accordingly, I don't have to either.

"I can give you half an hour," I said, rather ungraciously. "Where do you live?"

On the way there, I asked her who'd told her about me. She said she couldn't remember.

The daughter was a skinny, stupid-looking little thing, which made me wonder who the hell could be bothered; a question that would of course be answered very soon. I took the mother to one side. You do realise, I told her, that if I wipe this memory, she won't be able to identify the men or testify against them; they'll get off scot-free, and that's not right. She just looked at me. Fair enough. Justice (which doesn't exist) is not to be confused with retribution. Justice would be making it so that the bad thing had never even happened. Justice is mine, saith the Invincible Sun.

I sat down on a three-legged stool opposite the girl and stared at her until the side of her head melted and I could see in. There were the usual rows of shelves, with the memories stacked on them. No trouble at all finding the one I was after. It was right there in front of me. I reached for it and took it down.

—and there she was, the skinny girl, standing next to me. She had a long, thin nose that reminded me of someone, and no lobes to her ears. She was staring at me—not eye to eye, she was gazing at the side of my head. Get out of it, I shouted at her—I mouthed the words but could make no sound. Stop doing that. Get out of my mind. She turned her head and looked at me, frowning, as if I were logically impossible. She said something, but I couldn't hear it. Her lips were thin and practically colourless, and I couldn't read them. It's for your own good, you stupid girl, I tried to tell her. She couldn't understand me. She reached for the scroll in my hand, but I pulled it away. I could feel her looking through the wall of my skull. It hurt like hell. I yelled, and got out of there.

The girl had her eyes tight shut, and she was screaming. Her mother pulled me off the stool and dragged me away. She was shouting, stop it, what have you done to her? Then the girl stopped yammering; I pulled my arm out of the mother's sharklike grip and ran out into the street. People turned and looked at me. I kept running. I remember thinking, when He does it, they're grateful. I get yelled at. There's no justice.

––––––––––

The plan had been to spend the morning cruising elegantly round the various auctioneers and real-estate agents. I didn't do that. Instead, I went home, wedged my one chair against the door, and sat crouched in a corner.

The memory of the rape (which was bad enough, God knows) had somehow fused with the moment when I found the skinny girl standing next to me. I wanted to hide, but you can't when it's yourself you're trying to run away from. Just as well I'd dumped that sword, or I'd have tried to cut my own head off. Any damn thing, just to make it stop.

––––––––––

Which it did, of its own accord, a long and unquantifiable

amount of time later. What cured it, I think, was a little voice in my head, apparently unaffected by the mayhem going on all around (like the farmer in the valley just over the ridge from the battle, who goes on serenely plough- ing while thirty thousand men die, half a mile away) that kept repeating; I know that woman, I'm sure I've seen her before, I never forget a face—

And then I sort of slid into another of the memories I'd taken from the good-looking man the day before. This time it was a nice one. He was sitting on the grass beside a river—I knew the place, an old abandoned iron mine high up on the moor, sounds grim but actually it's beau- tiful when the heather's out and the sun's shining. He was with another man and two pretty girls, and they were all dressed in the gentrified walking outfits that were in fash- ion about twenty years ago. There was a big wicker bas- ket; cold chicken, ham, garlic sausage, fluffy white rolls; a stone bottle floated in the river to keep it cool, a string round its neck to keep it from floating away, anchored to a wooden peg driven into the turf of the bank. I made a joke (which I didn't quite catch); the girls laughed, but the other man scowled—he didn't like that I was amus- ing them, and that made me want to smile. He was my best friend and a brother officer, but all's fair in love and war.

Around noon, I suddenly remembered that I was still

hungry. I've never been so pleased to be hungry in all my life.

———————

To reconcile my unkempt appearance with my desire to buy an expensive house, I told them I was a gold miner just back from the Mesoge. I don't think they believed me but it was an acceptable lie; they recognised it, the way governments recognise each other without necessarily approving. I showed them a letter from the Social and Beneficent, which confirmed that I was indeed a rich man, whose funds would be available to draw on in nine days' time. They liked me ever so much more after that.

The first place they took me to see, I didn't even bother going inside. Sorry, I told them, but I don't have a dog. And if I did, I wouldn't be so cruel as to keep it cramped up in something that small.

The next place was just off the Park, opposite the side gate of the Baths of Genseric. There was a high brick wall with a tiny wicket gate in it; go through that and you're suddenly in this beautiful formal garden, with a fountain and little box-hedge-enclosed diamonds planted out in sweet herbs and lavender. The house itself was early Formalist, with those tiny leaded-pane windows and two ornate columns flanking the front door. The price they were asking seemed a trifle on the cheap side; it turned out they were acting as agents for the Treasury, the house having been confiscated from the estate of a recently executed traitor. I had, how shall I put it, certain connections with that case (here's a hint; they hanged the wrong man). Thanks but no thanks.

The third one was just right. It was on the riverbank; the main entrance was actually from a landing-stage, and we arrived by boat. As soon as I walked through the door I felt at home. There was something about the place that made me feel right somehow, as though I'd been away for too long but was back again where I ought to be. I sat down on the window seat in the back kitchen and looked out over the river. I could see a boat, one of those flat-bottomed barges they use for hauling lumber and ore down from the moors to the City. It lay low in the water, and gulls were mobbing the crew as they lounged and ate barley cakes in the bows. I grinned and reached for my tea.

Which wasn't there, of course, although my fingers closed with exact precision on where the tea-bowl should have been—where it had been, twenty-one years ago, when I sat in the bay window of my best friend's house, the second day of his first home leave from the war—

I jumped up, remembering to duck my head so as not to crack it against the overhanging beam, which I hadn't noticed when I sat down (but I knew it was there, just as I know where my fingers are) and ran out of the house. The agent was outside, leaning against a pillar, eating an apple. Not this one, I told him. He smiled. Of course not, he said. Let's go and look at something else.

The next day, the man from the Knights of Poverty took me out to see a place he was sure I'd like, about ten miles north of the city. True, it was just a farmhouse; but in the big hay meadow stood the derelict but still fundamentally sound shell of a fine old manor house. I could live in the farm while the big house was done up, which wouldn't take long (by an extraordinary coincidence, his brother-in-law the builder lived in the village) and then I'd have exactly the home I wanted, created to my precise specifications, for a tenth of what it'd have cost to buy anything similar that still had a roof. We saw the ruin first. It was a tall galleon of bleak, untidy stone rearing up out of a sea of nettles. It certainly had potential, the way a granite boulder is potentially a masterpiece of portrait sculpture. It looked as much like a house as I do, but the Knight assured me his brother-in-law would have it shipshape in ten minutes flat. Then we looked round the farmhouse; one big room downstairs, a combination bedroom and hayloft above it. I grew up in a smaller version. Oh, and there were a hundred and ninety acres of good pasture, if I was interested in that sort of thing. Five hundred angels. I offered him four and he accepted open-mouthed, as though he'd just cut open a fish and found a giant ruby. I asked him, who used to live in the big house? He didn't know. It was a long time ago, and everyone had died or moved away.

The best thing about living in the farmhouse was nobody knowing I was there. I had taken pains to leave no forwarding addresses, and I'd made the Knights promise they'd never heard of me, if anyone came asking.

The second best thing was the house itself, with its paved yard, three barns, well, and stable. I walked into the village and bought a dozen chickens; an old woman and a very young boy brought them on a handcart that afternoon, by which time I'd fixed up the end of the smallest barn as a poultry shed. I left the chickens pecking weeds out from between the flags in the yard and hiked out east to look for my neighbour; he turned out to be a short, broad, harassed-looking man about my age, who sold me a half-ton of barley and told his eldest boy to cart it over that evening. By nightfall, I had chicken-feed and chickens to feed it to; I ground a big cupful of the barley in a rusty hand-mill I found in the middle barn, to make bread for myself the next day. I'd forgotten how tiring it is working one of those things. After an hour, my arm and neck ached and I still had half the grain to do. I was happy, for the first time in years; relaxed, peaceful, as I'd assumed only a god could be.

Over the next two weeks I bought two dozen good ewes at the fair, and a pony and cart, and a dog. I was busy patching up the hedges and fences. The Knight's brother-in-law came asking for money. He found me in the long pasture, splitting rails out of a crooked ash I'd felled the previous day, and asked me if I knew where the owner was. Who? The rich city gent who'd bought the big house. Oh, him, I said, and sent him down to the farmhouse. He left a note. I wrote a reply and a draft on the Bank, walked down to the village when it was too dark to work, and slipped it under his door. Two days later I was driving the sheep to new pasture and happened to pass the ruin. It was almost invisible under new white pine scaffolding, like a city under siege. I gave it a wide berth.

That night the fox got in and killed all my chickens. I remember sitting cross-legged in the yard, surrounded by feathered wrecks, bawling like a child.

Then they tracked me down, and a carriage arrived to take me to the City. Get lost, I told the driver, I'm retired, I'm a gentleman of leisure now. He looked at my clothes and the hammer and fencing pliers stuck through my belt and the wire burns on my hands, and went away to report to his superiors.

Then the young man—the old man's son—rode out to see me. They needed me, he said. He understood that I'd given up regular practice, but he was sure I'd make an exception. The fee was a thousand angels. I'm retired, I said, I'm a gentleman farmer. I have all the money I could possibly want.

He looked at me as though I was mad. We need you, he said. Things have taken a turn for the worse. My father is seriously concerned.

He'd interrupted me while I was driving in a fence post. I'd been working since dawn, and the sledge felt like it weighed three hundredweight. I'm retired, I repeated. Sorry, but I don't do that stuff any more.

My father says you've got to come now, he said. Maybe I haven't made myself clear. This is important.

So's this, I told him. And I retired. Sorry.

He scowled at me. We've been doing some research,

he said. About you. We found out some interesting things. He grinned; it made him look like a dog. You've led an eventful life, haven't you?

I thought about smashing his skull with the hammer, and decided against it. Probably it was a weak decision. If I'd killed him and melted away into the countryside (wouldn't be the first time I'd done that) I'd have had to give up the money and the farm and my apotheosis, but I'd have been free and clear, for a little while. I could have gone anywhere, been anybody, done anything. A weak and tired decision; I traded freedom and infinite potential for a little comfort.

Who told you? I said.

He shook his head. I'm hardly likely to tell you, am I? Anyway, there it is. You can refuse if you like, but if you do, you'll regret it. Come on, he added. We can't afford to waste time.

I put it to him that blackmailing me would be a very bad idea, given that I knew enough about him and his father to destroy the entire world. But he just gave me an impatient look, because he knew as well as I did that if I went to the authorities, I wouldn't live long enough to testify; and, as a relatively new, arriviste god, with no friends or connections among the senior pantheon, my absence wouldn't arouse much comment.

He'd come in a covered two-seater chaise. It wasn't

designed to carry two people long distances on poor roads. I comfort myself with the reflection that he must have suffered even more than I did, every time we went over a pothole.

———————

Consider it this way. The present is a split second, so tiny and trivial as to be immaterial. Everything else, everything real and substantial, is a coral reef of dead split seconds, forming the islands and continents of our reality. Every moment is a brick in the wall of the past, building enormous structures that have identity and meaning, cities we live in. The future is wet shapeless clay, the present is so brief it barely exists, but the past houses and shelters us, gives us a home and a name; and the mortar that binds those bricks, that stops them from sliding apart into a nettle-shrouded ruin, is memory.

I had no way of knowing, of course, exactly which of my past misdemeanours he'd contrived to unearth. But—last time I counted, and that was a while back, thirty-six of them carried the death penalty in the relevant jurisdiction, and I'd long since lost count of the things I'd done which would land me in jail or the galleys or the hulks or the slate quarries if anyone ever brought them home to me. The issue is confused, of course, by all the crimes I remember vividly but didn't do; even so, I was and am uncomfortably aware that my past (so long as memory sustains it) isn't so much a city as a condemned cell. Don't get me wrong; I'm not fundamentally a bad person. They'll hang you for any damn thing in some of the places I've been, Boc Auxine or Perigeuna; failure to salute the flag, sneezing during the Remembrance Festival. But I've had my moments. As previously noted, no angel.

―――――――

Someone opened the chaise door and I poked my head out. Not somewhere I recognised, though it was fairly obvious what sort of place it was. Mile-high tenement blocks crowded round a little square yard; two single-storey sheds north and south, and in the middle a circle of black ash ringed with big sooty stones; to the right a fifty-gallon barrel with one charred side. You've got it; a wheelwright's yard, of which there are probably forty in the City, maybe more—the ruts in the streets are hard on wheels and axles. I guessed we weren't there to have the chaise fixed, however.

The young man led me into the shed on the north side. The shutters were down, but there was a big fire still glowing on the forge hearth. The old man was sitting awkwardly on an anvil, with five men standing behind him; they needed no explanation. Opposite the old man, kneeling on the hard stone floor, was a little thin man, anywhere between forty and fifty-five. He had a black eye and a cut lip, ugly bruise on his cheek, hair matted with blood from one of those scalp wounds that just keep on bleeding. He was nursing his left hand in his right; someone had flattened his fingertips on the anvil with a big hammer. He had that still, quiet look.

The old man glanced up as I came in, then turned his attention back to the poor devil kneeling on the floor. This man, he said, stole from us. He was a clerk in the counting-house, we looked after him, trusted him, and he stole from us. And he won't tell us what he's done with our money.

I looked at the clerk, who shook his head. It's not true, he said (it was hard to make out the words, his mouth was too badly damaged), I never stole anything. The young man rolled his eyes, as though the clerk were a naughty boy with jam round his mouth insisting he knew nothing about the missing cake.

Fine, I said, we can settle this quite easily. I braced myself; it was going to be a difficult, nasty job, and I was out of practice.

I did the old man first. I'm ashamed to admit that I was a bit cavalier about going in. I've found you can modulate—is that the word?—the level of discomfort you cause when you look through the side of someone's head; on this occasion, I didn't bother too much. The memories I wanted were easy enough to find—half of the things he'd found out about me weren't even true. I bundled them up, wiped the memory of the pain, and got out fast. Same for his son. Then I did the clerk. Then out again. By this time I was feeling shattered, sweat running down my face and inside my shirt, as though I'd just run up a steep hill with a hay bale hanging from each hand.

"He's telling the truth," I said. "He never stole from you, and he hasn't got your money."

The old man opened his mouth, then closed it again. The young man called me a liar and various other things; his father sighed and told him to be quiet.

The clerk's head had rolled forward onto his chest; he was asleep. "You'd better untie him and dump him in an alley somewhere," I went on. "I've taken away all his memories of what you've done to him, he'll wake up and have no idea how he got in this state, it'll save you having to kill him." I smiled. "Now, then," I said, "I don't think we discussed my fee. The usual rate?"

The old man gave me a puzzled look, then wrote out a draft for three hundred angels. I didn't argue. "Well," I said, "it's been a pleasure working for you, but as I told your son, I'm retired now, so we won't be seeing each other again. Rest assured you can rely on my discretion. Don't bother giving me a lift, I can walk."

I got out of there as quickly as I could, and headed straight for the Sword of Justice, simply because it was nearest and I badly needed a drink. So badly, in fact, that I stuck to black tea with honey and pepper, because some things you need you shouldn't always get. I was sipping it when a man I used to know came up and told me they'd got a game going out back, if I was interested.

I looked at him and grinned. "Sorry," I said, "I'm broke. Look at me," I added.

He did so, noting the farm clothes and the worn-out boots. "Screw you, then," he replied pleasantly, and left me in peace.

———————

How was it, I hear you ask, that I came to develop my unique talent and establish a career as the Empire's leading consulting memory engineer?

It's a classic success story. There I was, an ignorant farm boy on the run from the law, turning up in the big city with nothing but the rags on his back and a dream of a better life. An early but significant demonstration of my powers came about when hunger drove me to the back door of the old Industry and Enterprise in Sheep

Street—remember it? It's gone now, of course, pulled down to make space for the new cattle pens. The door was open, and I could see through into the kitchen, where they were roasting chickens on a spit. There didn't seem to be anybody about, so I nipped in and helped myself.

I was cheerfully stuffing my face when the landlord loomed up out of the shadows and kicked me halfway across the room. Then he picked up a cleaver. I swear it was instinct; I stared right through his skull, picked out the sight of me tiptoeing in and grabbing a chicken, and darted back out again. There was the landlord, cleaver in hand, puzzled frown on face. Who the hell are you? he asked me. Got any work? I answered. No, get lost. I nodded (I'd stuck the chicken down the front of my shirt) and headed back into the street as fast as I could go.

For someone who'd had to work for his living, this episode was a revelation to me; a flawless modus operandi, fully formed and perfected, like suddenly waking up one morning to find that you'd learned the silversmith's trade overnight, in a dream. I refined it a bit, of course. I know, they say *if it ain't broke don't fix it,* but I modified the original pattern to leave out the getting-kicked-across-the-room stage, and in the event it worked just as well without it. Instead, I'd go into teashops when there were no other customers, eat and drink as much as I liked, then cause the owner to forget me completely. Same with dosshouse-keepers and landladies of furnished accommodation; as soon as they asked me for rent, they'd never seen me before in their lives. I got into a few scrapes, it's true, but that's all done and forgotten about now. In due course, I refined my business model and started getting jobs that actually paid money; eventually, lots of money, which somehow never stayed with me very long, but that's not the point. I was a success. I made something of myself, and there's not many men from my background who can say that.

––––––––––––

So why, I hear you ask, did I turn my back on all that, a lifetime of achievement, not to mention the money, in order to go scurrying back to my grubby roots and relapse into peasant farming?

Actually, I should think that was obvious. I was terrified. Ever since I'd done that job on the girl who was raped, I knew something was terribly wrong. I'd tried to figure out what had happened, couldn't—no matter. I'm not a scholar or a scientist, just an honest artisan practising his trade. But when the trade gets dangerous and not worth the risk, I stop. Simple; if I don't go back there, it can't hurt me. And I was horribly sure that if I did go back, I'd get hurt.

I could remember it all perfectly; the skinny girl, standing next to me. She had a long, thin nose, and no lobes to her ears. She was staring at me—not eye to eye, she was gazing at the side of my head. Get out of it, I shouted at her—I mouthed the words but could make no sound. Stop doing that. Get out of my mind. She turned her head and looked at me, frowning, as if I were a spelling mistake. She said something, but I couldn't hear it. Her lips were thin and practically colourless, and I couldn't read them. It's for your own good, you stupid girl, I tried to tell her. She couldn't understand me. She reached for the scroll in my hand, but I pulled it away. I could feel her looking through the wall of my skull. It hurt like hell. I yelled, and got out quick—

———

So what's the chance, I kept asking myself, that there's someone else out there with the same knack or talent I've got; a skinny girl, nobody really, but she can see through the walls of skulls into the library inside? Except that wasn't what I'd encountered, was it? I met her inside her own head, conscious of me; she'd tried to get at my memories, but I'd been too quick for her and got away before she could break in. Conclusion: she could do what I can do, but there was more to it than that. She was aware of me gatecrashing her mind; she was actually there, in person, and nearly managed to snatch the scroll out of my hand.

And still only young, twenty or so; not much older than I was when I started. Give her a few years to come to terms with her ability and put on a bit of mental muscle—what other tricks could she do, I wondered? What sort of monster had I blundered into?

———————

I owed her a drink, of course. If it hadn't been for the scare she'd put into me, I'd never have found the strength to quit the job and get out of the City. That change was definitely an improvement, no question at all about it.

I cashed the old man's draft and got them to write a letter of credit to the Social and Beneficent; another couple of hundred couldn't do any harm, after all, even if I was highly unlikely ever to need it. Then I caught the carrier's cart to my village and walked the rest of the way. It had been raining, and the wet grass soaked my trousers up to the knees. I walked past the ruin—they'd roofed it over with wooden shingles, over which I'd specified a single continuous sheet of burnished copper, but they hadn't got round to that yet. I peered at it from a distance, too far away to make out what the builders' men were saying, and cut through the woods to get home. The smell of the wet grass was wonderful. It was nearly dark by then. The back door was slightly ajar, just as I'd left it. I went inside and groped for the lamp and the tinderbox. I was just about to wind the tinderbox handle when light filled the room.

Two of them; I can picture them to this day—one lifting the shutter of a dark lantern, the other rising gracefully to his feet and levelling the crossbow he'd been cradling on his knees. He was the one who messed it all up, of course, because as he stood up he got between his target and the light, giving me plenty of time to back out and slam the door in his face; I felt it quiver as the bolt hit it. I was almost as stupid as he was. I wasted a good second looking round for something to wedge the door with, instead of legging it straightaway into the friendly, conspiratorial dark. But I got smart as soon as I felt his weight slam against the door; I let go, allowing him to sprawl out and trip over his feet, while I scampered across the yard toward the hay barn. The only reason I went that way was a vague memory of where I'd left a hayfork, which was the only weapon I had that wasn't in the house.

The trouble with a vague memory is it doesn't help you find things in the pitch dark. Furthermore, while I was groping about in the hay, I trod on that damned loose floorboard, the one that creaks like a soul in torment. The sound carried wonderfully in the still night air. I froze; not tactics, terror. Then I heard the scrape of a hobnail on the slate lintel.

———————

It reminded me of a night, many years earlier, when I'd crept through a dark garden towards the wall of a house and looked up at a narrow window. The architect who built that house had no daughters, or he wouldn't have allowed the window of the best east-facing bedroom, looking out over the rose garden, to be so easily accessible by drainpipe.

I was quite athletic in those days, but just as clumsy as I am now. The heel of my boot dragged on the stone windowsill, making a noise that sounded like morning shift in the slate quarries. I froze and counted to twenty; her mother's maid slept in the next room, and was no friend of mine. But twenty came and went, no banging doors or raised voices. I hauled myself over the sill and got my feet down on a good, discreet Vesani rug.

But something was wrong. She should have been there. I was alone in someone else's house. Suddenly, I felt like a burglar.

Fortuitously, I knew about burglary, thanks to a paying customer. I knew how to walk quietly, and what to watch out for. I crept through the dressing room into her bedroom. It was dark. I knew its geography, of course. I have a blind man's memories of how to navigate in the dark. I found the bed, and my fingertips told me it was made up. I stood there, feeling incredibly stupid. Then the door opened, and the light almost blinded me.

I should explain that I'd been away for nearly six months, for my health. I hadn't dared write, and all the time I was away I'd been out of my mind with worry. The first thing I did when I got back was leave the agreed sign—a hand-and-flower, chalked on the foot of the sundial at the end of the rose garden; when I came back the next night, her countersign was there, with two crosses, meaning *in two days' time*. So she was still there, still wanted to see me; but her room was empty.

Framed in the light was a man I knew only too well, though we'd never met face to face or spoken to each other. At that time, her father was a senator and a wealthy merchant, doing extremely well in the cotton and linen business; this was several years before the crash came and it turned out that the only money he had was what he'd embezzled from Party funds. He was a big man, bald, with the arms and shoulders of a country blacksmith, and his attitude towards me, as far as I could gather, was basically agnostic; he couldn't quite bring himself to believe that I existed, but he had lurking suspicions. He was alone, but all that signified was a sensible disinclination to share the next few minutes with any witnesses.

I'd already turned to run for it, but he said, "No, wait," and there was something in the way he said it—not anger, just sadness. I stayed where I was and he came up close and held the lamp so he could see my face. "You're shorter than I expected," he said.

"Where is she?"

For a moment I thought he was going to go for me. The little, isolated part of my mind that arranges tactical details was busy taking note of the fact that he was holding the lamp in his right hand and his left hand was empty; no weapon, so either he was unarmed or he'd have to shift the lamp to his left to draw; or if he planned on killing me with his bare hands, he'd have to lead with his left, and his feet were all wrong for that, unless he was a natural southpaw—But then he shook his head, and the look on his face made me go cold. "She's dead," he said.

It's so easy to say; in that moment, I died. Grand overstatement. Melodrama. I wish I had the words, but I don't.

He went on: "There was a problem with the pregnancy. It was blood poisoning."

All I could do was repeat: "Pregnancy."

He made this noise. It was a big, cold laugh. "You didn't know?"

"No. I—" I ran out of words and just stood there.

"Ah." He nodded slightly. "Interesting. She assumed you'd guessed and run out on her because of it. Well, it killed her. It took a long time. They gave her poppy extract, but the pain was—" He stopped and shrugged. "You killed my daughter."

This tactical part of my mind—I wonder, do other people have the same thing, or is it just me? If it's just me, is it somehow connected with the special thing I do? I've often wondered. In any event, at that moment it was busy again. It was telling me: his wife, her mother, died five years ago, and he has no close family; I could wipe her out of his memory and spare him the pain, it was the least I could do. But that wouldn't work. He was a man in public office, with about a million acquaintances, all of them properly sympathetic. It wouldn't really help matters if I got him a reputation for having been driven insane by grief.

"I was going to kill you," he said. He was looking straight at me, the way an arrow looks at a target. "But I think I'll let you live. It'd be crueller."

He was right about that. Being dead is bad enough. Being dead and still having to walk around and eat is so much worse.

———————

Hence the sudden and immediate twist of pain when I heard that nail-on-stone noise. No bad thing, really; it prevented me from ignoring the sound or mistaking it for something else. Saved my life, actually. Now there's irony.

My tactical planner was giving me instructions; get down, keep still, make yourself small. I had no weapon and chances were the owner of the hobnailed boot was a much better fighter than me, but I had the advantage of the dark; I knew where he was, but he didn't know where I was. He was, of course, between me and the door. I've been in worse situations.

Then I had a stroke of luck. He uncovered his dark lantern. He saw me and I saw him.

I went in through the side of his head like a sling-stone. As I'd assumed, the old man had sent him; my reluctance and intention to retire had made me an unacceptable risk, no longer outweighed by my potential usefulness. Fine. I wiped that; then, in an access of spite of which I am not proud, I wiped a whole lot more— his name, most of his past, more or less everything in easy reach. When I came out of his head, he was standing there looking stupid. There was a hay rake leaning up against the wall. I grabbed it and broke it over his head. I felt sorry for him, and ashamed of myself.

He'd dropped the lantern, but it hadn't gone out; a lit lantern on the floor of a hay barn is nobody's friend. I grabbed it, and then it did go out. I went to the door and threw it away. One down.

I stood in the doorway and tried to be sensible. Defeating one hired man wasn't victory in any meaningful sense. If the old man had decided it was time for me to die, I could defeat a thousand of his footsoldiers in tense little duels and still be no safer. My own stupid fault. By buying a house and putting down roots, I'd made myself an easy target—one of the very few stupid things I'd never done before. I don't know. Maybe there's a secret part of me that won't be satisfied until I've completed the set.

Time to go. As I walked quietly up to the road, I cursed myself for cashing that two-hundred-angel draft. It'd be suicide to go anywhere near the Social and Beneficent, or even to write a draft; they'd track me down and that'd be that. My only hope lay in anonymity and distance.

I started walking. About a week later, I stopped and asked where I was. They looked at me as if I were crazy and said, Scheria. Just my luck.

———————

Don't get me wrong. There are worse places than Scheria. Four of them, at least.

I never had the time or the energy to learn a musical instrument; but I had the unhappy privilege of attending the great Clamanzi in his last illness, which was horribly exacerbated by memories of how badly he'd treated his wife. The poor man only had days to live, and it was certain he'd never play the flute again. It wasn't really stealing, more a case of rescuing a glorious thing and keeping it safe.

Partly out of respect, I'd never even picked up a flute since that day; but it was all there, in my head. My tactical adviser suggested that the old man's people wouldn't be looking for a travelling musician. And, whatever their other faults as a nation, the Scherians are fond of music.

I'm ashamed to say, I stole the flute. I heard its music as I was walking down a village street. Pretty tune, I thought; then it stopped, and maybe its beauty reminded me of Clamanzi, I don't know. I waited; it started again, and I traced it to a house in the corner of a little square. I went away and came back after dark. The blind man I mentioned just now helped me find the flute—it had been left lying around on the kitchen table, some people are just so careless. My flute now.

To practice, I walked up into the hills. As well as the flute, I'd found a new loaf on that kitchen table, and there are plenty of sweet-water springs draining off the peat. I allowed myself three days to learn the flute. Took me about half an hour, in the event. The rest of the time I took to eat that loaf, I just enjoyed myself, playing music.

I say *myself*; I can't really claim any credit. I'm the first to admit, I don't have an artistic bone in my body. So please don't make the mistake of thinking that listening to me was like listening to Clamanzi. I had the fingering, the breath control, the education, the technique—but no passion, no soul. Correction: I had my soul, which is a pretty inferior example of the type and certainly not something you'd want to listen to. No angel; I think we've established that. But I could pipe a tune, as well as most and better than some, and a piper can always earn a few stuivers in Scheria. Not that there's much in those parts you'd want to spend it on.

The hell with it; I walked to the next town, sat down in front of the mercantile, and started to play. Not even a hat at my feet—I didn't actually possess a hat—just music, for its own sake. To begin with, people were reluctant, because there was no obvious place to drop their coins. But once two or three stuivers were gathered together in a little cluster that ceased to be a problem. The store owner came out and I thought he was going to move me on; instead, he brought me out a bowl of tea and a loaf of bread, quietly so as not to disturb me. I only stopped when my lips got sore, by which time the pile of coins was too big to hold comfortably in one hand. Best part of a quarter angel; more than a skilled man earns in a week.

I slept, by invitation, in the storekeeper's comfortable hayloft, and started playing again as soon as it was light. It helped that I can remember every tune I ever heard. On the third day it rained; but that wasn't a problem, because the local lord-of-the-manor sent a cart for me. He had guests for dinner, and if I wasn't busy . . . A month later, I'd moved to Cerauno, which is the third largest city in Scheria, and was playing indoors, to people who'd come specially to hear me, and who handed in their coins at the door rather than dropping them on the ground. Three months later, I was rich. Again.

I seem to have this knack of hauling myself up by my bootstraps, usually when my mind is on other things.

Practically every night in Cerauno I dreamed about the skinny girl. Sometimes she was in the dark looking for me, with a knife; sometimes I met her in the street or beside the river. Sometimes she had a knife, other times it would be a rope or an axe. The one constant was that she wanted to kill me.

I heard the news of the coup back home from the ambassador himself, no less, at a reception. He confessed that he was terrified at the thought of being recalled, since he was clearly identified with the old regime. I asked him who was behind it all; he looked round to make sure nobody was listening, and whispered a few names. Two of them (father and son) I recognised.

I reminded myself that I was a professional, and my clients' secrets were sacrosanct, even if the clients in question had sent assassins to murder me. If I were you, I told the ambassador, I'd stay here where it's safe. Those clowns won't last long, sooner or later they'll cut each others' throats and everything will go back to normal. Don't go back, whatever you do. He gave me a sad smile. My wife and daughter are still there, he said, in the City.

I thought about that while pretending to sip my tea, though the bowl was empty. If he refused to go back, they'd kill his family. If he went back, they'd kill him and his family as well, because now they were in power they could afford to be particular about loose ends. I know; it was only my opinion, and what do I know about high-level politics? But I'd come to like the ambassador; he'd fallen asleep in the front row of one of my recitals, on a night when I was particularly uninspired—he clearly had taste, and I like that in a man.

He turned away to grab one of those rice-cakes-filled-with-pureed-seaweed that the Scherians fondly imagine are edible. I stared at the side of his head, and then he turned back. He was frowning.

Tell me, ambassador, I said. Are you married?

He looked at me as if I'd just asked him for the square root of seven. No, he said.

I smiled at him. If I were you, I said, I'd stay here in Scheria where it's safe. He nodded. I might just do that, he said.

As soon as I could, I left the reception, went home to my comfortable lodgings in fashionable Peace Square, and was violently sick. I can only assume it was the pureed seaweed.

I'd been in Scheria for about six months when I started hearing rumours. News from the Old Country was hard to come by; my only reliable source was my friend the ambassador (Scheria didn't recognise the new regime, so he stayed on; he was invited to receptions, but had to borrow money to live on) and all he knew came from refugees and exiles. Apart from what he told me, I heard the usual wild and improbable stuff, a mixture of impossible atrocity stories and political gossip, scurrilous in tone and often biologically impossible. But just occasionally I heard something that rang true. For instance: I heard that the society charlatan who used to claim he could read minds had mysteriously disappeared just before the coup, but lately there was a new mind-reader who'd taken over his old practice; she was in favour with the regime, who made no secret of her supposed powers. They used her for interrogations and to administer a particularly terrifying form of punishment—artificially induced amnesia. The victim, so the rumour went, was left with no memories whatsoever, not even his name. It was the proverbial fate worse than death, and apparently the new government kept her extremely busy. Her? Oh, yes, my informants assured me, this mind-reader's a woman, actually just a young girl, but nasty as a sackful of adders. Also, they've put a price on the old mind-reader's head; ten thousand angels dead, twenty-five thousand if they get him alive. Of course, it's all nonsense, but—

And my mother used to tell me I'd never amount to anything. Twenty-five thousand angels. It's enough to make your head spin. No human being could conceivably be worth that. It made me wish I still had a family, so I could turn myself in and make them all rich.

———————————

I remember the first time I saw her.

I remember it two ways; in one version, I'm sitting on a low wall, talking to my best friend. The other way, I'm standing; apart from that, it's the same, up to the point where I say, "I think I know her brother," in a soft whisper. From then on, the two versions diverge.

In one version, I just stand there, bashful and hopeless. In the other, I go up to her, introduce myself. She gives me that look nice girls are supposed to give to importunate strangers. Then I ask if her brother is so-and-so, who was at the Studium at such-and-such a time. Why, yes, she says, and smiles, and he's mentioned you.

In the other version, I reflect bitterly on my lack of education, which meant I'd never been at some fancy school with the brothers of pretty girls. Meanwhile I watch my best friend exercise his legendary charm, and think; oh well.

Footnotes: at this time, I'd been in the City for just under a year. I'd started exercising my talent in a controlled and profitable manner; I was making a lot of money, and spending it on playing the part of an affluent merchant's son—no attempt to hide the taint of trade, but a surprising number of genuine young noblemen are happy to associate with parvenus, if they're witty and presentable and prepared to buy the drinks and pay for the damage. Nobody asked me searching questions about my antecedents, because it was assumed they couldn't possibly be more disgraceful than a rich wine-merchant for a father. My friend had recently left the military academy and was loosely associated with a good regiment (but not in such a way as to cut unduly into his free time).

She had a friend, who I didn't like much. The four of us went to various social events. It wasn't a happy time for me.

The news that I'd been supplanted in my profession didn't bother me much, per se; I had no intention of resuming my practice if I could possibly avoid it. I much preferred flute-playing, and Scheria was starting to grow on me, like some sort of lichen. It was my supplanter herself who bothered me; that and the price on my head. If I was safe anywhere, it was Scheria—war hadn't been formally declared, but the border was closed, and one of my compatriots would've been noticed and dealt with very quickly; the Scherians are good at that sort of thing. Even so, twenty-five thousand angels has a sort of inner momentum that tends to transcend politics. One thing was certain. I didn't dare go back and investigate this woman, even if I'd wanted to.

―――――――

Instead, I played the flute. I'm not sure what got into me. Maybe it was the worry and the stress, or perhaps it was just Clamanzi getting used to my mouth and fingers. I got better and better. It helped that I was encouraged to tackle a wider repertoire—the great Scherian classics, Gorgias, Procopius, Cordusa; you can't put an infinite amount of soul into the folk tunes I'd picked up back home, but if you put together Clamanzi's technique and Procopius's flute sonatas, there's a sort of alchemical re-action that refuses to be confined by the spiritual poverty of the intermediary, even when he's me. Also, people who know about music say that the great performer draws on his experience, which is just another word for memories; of those I had plenty. Even the greatest virtuoso—even Clamanzi—can only draw on his own experience, which limits him. Unless he happens to have a head stuffed full of other people's lives, sorrows, joys, wickedness, weakness, and misery. I reached a point where I could let the music and the memories talk to each other. A hundred strangers provided the soul, Clamanzi operated the keys, I stood there while it happened, bowed when it was over, and took the money. I remember one reception, where I'd played for a bunch of ambassadors and ministers. Some fool came up to me, an old man, he looked like he'd been crying. He told me he'd heard the great Clamanzi play that sonata twenty years ago and had avoided hearing it since, because he was afraid to spoil the memory; but I had been better than Clamanzi, I'd found new depths, new resonances—

I'm afraid I was quite rude to him.

———————

There was one piece I flatly refused to play; Chirophon's *Lyrical Dances*, which was what the band played at a dance we all went to, around the time my best friend's regiment was posted south. It was while they were playing the second movement and the four of us were sitting it out on the veranda that I realised how much she loved him. I remember there was a beautiful glass decanter on the table; I looked at it and saw that if I broke it on the side of the table, I could cut his throat with the sharp edge of the neck before he had a chance to defend himself. I reached for it, my fingertips registered the smooth, cold surface; and I realised that there was a better way. Which is how I come to have his memories of her as well as my own. On the way back from the dance I stole them all; and the next day his regiment marched for the southern frontier. A month later he wrote to me; he was getting love letters from some female he'd never heard of— hot stuff, he said, you had to wear gloves to read them. He thought it was a huge joke, and should he write back? Write care of me, I replied; I'll deliver the letter and take a look at her for you. I don't know if he ever got that, because he was killed very soon afterwards.

The politics took a turn for the worse; enough to scare the Scherians into peace talks. A high-level delegation from the new regime would visit Scheria in the hope of preventing further escalation, and all that sort of thing. Naturally, there would be events, receptions. Naturally, I would be hired to play for them.

I got as far as packing a bag. Two bags, five—I realised I had far too much stuff I couldn't bear to be parted from, which was another way of saying that this time, I wasn't prepared to run away.

So I did the next best thing. I went to see my friend the

director of the Conservatory—in Scheria, the country's top musician is an ex efficio member of the Council of State, can you believe that? He was pleased to see me, sent for tea and honeycakes. "You saved me a job," he said. "I need to talk to you about the gala recital for the peace delegation."

I gave him a weak grin. "It's sort of about that," I said. "I can't do it."

He looked at me as though I'd just cut off his fingers. "Not funny," he said. I took a deep breath. "There are some things about me that maybe you ought to know," I told him.

And I explained. The story of my life. He sat perfectly still until I'd finished, and for a moment or so after that. Then he said, "But you haven't actually done anything wrong in Scheria."

I frowned. "Not yet."

"Don't mess with me," he snapped. "Since you got here, you've been a blameless, productive member of society. Yes? I need you to tell me the truth."

I nodded. "Apart from lying about who I am."

"That's not a crime," he said quickly, "unless you're on oath. So, the plain fact is, in Scheria you're clean."

I nodded. "Like that matters," I said. "Weren't you listening? As far as this delegation's concerned, I'm an enemy of the State. Also, I have information about two of the delegates that would kill them very dead if it ever got loose. Think about that."

He thought, though not for very long. "You wouldn't consider—"

"No. I'm definite on that. I don't tell."

He shrugged. "Before you go, do me a favour and make me forget you told me that, because it's my duty as a Counsellor to go to my colleagues and inform them that you have vital information that could win us the war, and all they have to do is torture you till you spit it out." He frowned. "You can really do that? That's amazing."

For a moment I didn't know what to say. "Thanks," I said. "But the point remains. As soon as they see me, they'll hit the roof. They'll assume—"

Suddenly he grinned. "Yes," he said. "Won't they just." He leaned forward and gave me a slap on the back that loosened three teeth. "How does it feel to be a secret weapon?"

It goes to show how stress mucks up your intellect; I hadn't seen it in that light before. "All right," I conceded. "But the moment that old devil sets eyes on me, my life won't be worth spit."

"We'll protect you." He nodded several times; habit of his. "Oh, you bet we will." He stopped and shook himself like a wet dog; I saw he was sweating, but he was better now. "Right," he said, "that's that dealt with. Onwards.

I was thinking, we start off with the Nicephorus quartet in C."

I went home—I had a nice place, opposite the Power and Glory Stairs—bolted the door, shuttered the windows, and lit the lamp. The first thing I saw was this mirror.

I bought it for half an angel, and I got a bargain; a genuine silver-backed glass mirror, Mezentine, about three hundred years old, there's only five or six in all of Scheria. The man who sold it to me grinned; present for the wife? Daughter? Girlfriend? I just smiled at him. I bought a mirror—the best that money could buy—to remind myself of something.

It was not long after she died, and I was called out to a surgeon, a household name. I can't tell you what it was about; not relevant. But in his house he had a mirror, a cheap brass-plate job, entirely out of place in his sumptuously decorated home. He saw me looking at it and told me the story; how, when he was a young Army sawbones, he got caught up in some actual fighting and took an arrow in the gut. He knew that unless he got the loathsome thing out quick, he'd be dead; also that there was nobody competent to do the job within thirty miles. So he set up that mirror where he could see it clearly, and operated on himself. He nearly killed himself, and he was sick as a dog for a month, but he survived, and had kept the mirror ever since, to remind himself that he was a genius for whom anything was possible.

And that, of course, set me thinking.

I was in the money at that time, so I bought myself a mirror; silver-backed glass, Mezentine, about three hundred years old, I paid twenty angels for it at an auction. I hired a carpenter to build a special cradle for it, so it could be swivelled about and adjusted to exactly the angle I wanted. Then, one night, I barred all the doors and windows and lit a hundred oil lamps—I wanted to be able to see what I was doing. I had no idea if what I planned on doing was possible—just like my client the surgeon, I guess; as with him, though, it was a matter of life and death, because I knew I couldn't carry on much longer, not with those memories inside my head.

I fiddled with the mirror until I had a clear view of the side of my own head. Then I stared, really hard; and I was in.

Exactly the same usual thing; a library, with shelves of scrolls. I knew, as I always do, which one to reach for. I picked it out, unrolled it. The page was blank.

Two days later, I sold the mirror. I got thirty angels for it, from a collector. Born lucky, I guess.

My friend the director and I eventually compromised on the Procopius concerto and the overture to *The Triumph of Compassion* (the Euxinus arrangement, not the Theodotus). I cancelled all my engagements for a week, and practiced till I could barely stand up. Not that I needed to, but it helped me feel like I was doing something. I'm guessing that, to this day, there's a company of the Third Lancers who cover their ears and whimper every time the band strikes up the *Triumph* overture; the poor devils ordered to guard me night and day must've heard the wretched thing a couple of hundred times.

(In case you're wondering, I didn't wipe my friend's memory after all; he got squeamish. He said he'd rather change his mind than have someone change it for him. I was mildly offended, but made nothing of it. I figure a friend has the right to offend you at least once.)

The concert was held in the auditorium of the Silver Star Temple, my second favourite after the Imperial; I wondered why, since it seats less than a thousand, until I remembered that at the Silver Star, there's an underground passage from the green room straight to the stage; the performers are out of sight of the audience until the screens actually come down. At the Imperial, you walk down the main aisle, and a man with a knife who didn't care about his future could have a go at you, and there'd be nobody to stop him. The choice of venue was considerate, but mildly terrifying; but the acoustic at the Silver Star is just right for the Procopius, especially the slow second movement.

The other thing about the stage at the Silver Star is that you're quite high up; which means you're on a dead level sight line with the best seats in the house (six rows from the front)—you can see them and they can see you. I remember peering out into the sea of faces just before I took my stand. I found them quite easily: the old man and his son. They were talking to each other, heads turned, not looking at the stage. Then, as I lifted the flute to my lips, the old man looked up and saw me, and he went white as a sheet. Then it was my cue, six bars in, and I forgot about everything else and started to play.

Clamanzi was at the top of his form that day. Actually, I don't rate the *Triumph* overture all that much—melodrama—but the Procopius is one of the supreme achievements of the human race (so very strange, that a really nasty piece of work like Procopius could have produced something so sublime) and I defy anybody who claims to be any better than an animal not to be completely carried away by it. I wasn't really aware of anything else until I'd played that last long string of dying thirds. Then, when the music stopped, in the split second of dead silence you always get before the applause starts, I sort of woke up and looked down at the audience. I was looking for the old man and his son, but my attention was distracted. I saw another familiar face, in the row above them.

Familiar in more than one sense . . .

Familiar, because I'd seen her before; once in the flesh, more times than I could count in dreams. But also familiar, because for the first time I realised who she reminded me of. It was the way she was sitting, the angle of her face, slightly away, chin slightly lifted. Nobody could ever call the skinny girl a beauty, but at that angle the resemblance was unmistakable.

———————

I can't remember how I got off the stage or back to the green room, but I remember sitting in a corner refusing tea and wine, and my friend the director bounding up to me like a friendly dog and yapping at me—wonderful, amazing, all the superlatives, except that he actually meant them; and especially the *Triumph,* my God, I never realised a human being could play like that. I frowned at him. I couldn't remember having played the *Triumph* overture—the Procopius, yes, but everything after that was just a blur. I muttered something or other and told him I'd like to be left in peace, please. He wasn't offended. Of course, he said, and made sure nobody spoke to me.

She was here; well, why was I surprised? Naturally, the enemy would bring their secret weapon. I had enough confidence in the Scherian authorities to assume that they knew what she could do and had taken the necessary measures to make sure she didn't do it to anybody who mattered—except that I'd been up there on stage, with her staring at me. A moment of panic; then I was able to reassure myself. I could remember every memory I'd acquired during my time with the old man and his son—

Presumably. But how the hell would I know?

No; be logical. I could remember things that would get their necks stretched in two minutes flat; therefore, she hadn't been at me. Quick mental geometry; how far was the stage from the eighth row of the auditorium? I didn't actually know; and for me, distance isn't really a problem, I can see through a man's head at any distance where I can clearly make out his face. But maybe the girl had problems with distance, maybe she was shortsighted. She had that slight squint, which would fit. And her mother . . .

I caught myself thinking that before I realised the implications; *her mother was short-sighted too,* when I knew her, twenty years ago.

Except that I'd met her mother, whom I'd never seen before (and I never forget a face); and the other woman had died twenty years ago, in childbirth.

I remember, I was alone in the green room by that stage, though presumably there was a half-company of guards outside in the corridor. I closed my eyes and tried to think. But my father and mother never showed any signs, perish the thought.

And then I reflected; be all that as it may, the reason she's here is to hurt you, of that you can be certain. And that takes priority over all other considerations. Doesn't it?

About twenty. Any age between nineteen and twenty-three. I've always been hopeless at guessing women's ages.

———

I slept badly—nightmares—and awoke to find that I'd been awarded an extra thousand angels, the Order of the Headless Spear, and full Scherian citizenship by a grateful Council. Well, I thought, that's nice.

My friend the director was in meetings all morning, but he made time to come and see me.

"That girl," I said, before he could sit down. "The one with the delegation. Have you any idea who she is?"

He nodded grimly. "We objected," he said, "but they insisted. It was a deal-breaker. But she's not allowed in to any of the sessions."

"She's here to kill me," I said.

He blinked. I could tell he believed me. "She couldn't get past the guards," he said.

I sighed. "You don't understand how it works," I told him. "She could get past an army. And you'd have fifty thousand soldiers who couldn't remember their own names."

He hadn't thought of that. "What can we do?"

I shrugged. "No idea," I said.

He frowned. Then he looked up. "We can poison her," he said.

He wasn't joking. "You can't." I'd spoken very quickly. "You'd start a war."

"There's poisons and poisons," he replied, and I felt cold all over. "All right, maybe not kill her. But a really bad stomach upset—"

In spite of everything I couldn't help laughing, at the thought of it.

"Trust me," he went on, "I've had a dicky tummy for years, while it's happening you simply can't think about anything else. A really bad dose of the shits will neutralise any power on Earth. We've got a man at Intelligence who specialises in that sort of thing. Leave it with me, it'll be just fine."

———————

He dosed the lot of them, for good measure. My guess is, he dressed it up in a dish of the notorious Scherian pork terrine, a national delicacy that'll do for anybody who hasn't been brought up on it since childhood. The rest of the delegation was up and about after a day or so. The girl (my friend reported cheerfully) had taken it particularly hard, probably because she was so thin and delicate, and would be confined to the shithouse for at least a week.

Woe to the conquered, I thought. Less extreme than killing her, as effective, considerably less humane.

———————

Except that it did kill her. The delegation withdrew from the negotiations for a whole day without any explanation, then announced that one of their advisers, a young woman, had contracted food poisoning and sadly passed away. It would have been her wish, they said, that the negotiations proceed; and so they proceeded.

There was a bleak little funeral, which I insisted on attending, though I had no right to do so—except, possibly, that the body they were burying was my daughter, and of course I couldn't tell anyone that. My daughter, killed on my orders, for the single reason that she took after her father. Possibly. No way of proving it, naturally. And that which can't be proven can't be regarded as true.

But I saw them set up a long wooden box on a trestle, stack logs all round it, splash around some oil and apply fire. There was that unmistakable roast-pork smell, which they try and mask with scenty stuff, but it never really works. The old man and his son were there, of course. They kept looking at me. It occurred to me, later, that I could've wiped their heads there and then, and been rid of them. Later. At the time, I was preoccupied with other things.

———————

They postponed the war, bless them; it would happen one day, inevitably as the leaves fall from the trees, but it wouldn't be soon. There was another concert, followed by a reception. I stood in a corner, trying to be invisible. Sure enough, the old man and his son headed straight for me.

You haven't told anyone. It was a statement of fact, which I confirmed. I pointed out that they'd sent men to kill me, driven me from my own country, and put a fortune on my head. They acknowledged as much, and warned me to keep my mouth shut and never, ever go home. They managed to make me feel as if it were all my fault. But they didn't mention the skinny girl, and neither did I.

The head of the delegation, who was also the provisional head of the provisional government (call him the provisional dictator) made a point of congratulating me on my performance and issuing a standing invitation to perform in the City, any time I felt like it. Clearly the old man and his son were as good at keeping secrets as me.

Then they went home; and I was mortally afraid that I'd lose my guards—they were picked men from the Prefect's Battalion, and there were probably other things they should have been doing. But my friend the director made out a case for me being a national treasure—I was eligible, apparently, now I was a citizen—which entitled me to maximum security, in case I was stolen, defaced, vandalised, or damaged. He made loads of jokes about it afterwards, which I managed to take in good part. I went back to work, to full houses and embarrassing applause; I didn't mind. I was playing better than ever, and enjoying every minute of it. As for money—I can honestly say I lost interest in it, the way fish aren't particularly interested in the sea.

I moved; from the centre of town out to the northern suburbs, where you could look out of your window and see meadows and woods. I never had time to do more than look at them. On the rare occasions when I was at home, I was totally occupied in learning and practising new pieces, or rehearsing with orchestras in the massive barn I'd had built in the grounds. People talked about me; they found it strange that I never did anything besides work, no time for pleasures, no wine, no women. I never tried to explain to anyone, understandably enough.

It was late one night. I'd been up since dawn, going through a new concerto I'd commissioned from a promising young composer. A wonderful thing; the more I played it, the more I found in it, and it struck me that if I hadn't existed, if I'd never been born and never lived a life that brought me to that place at that time in exactly that way, it might never have been written. The young man, almost obscenely talented, was only interested in the money, which he said he needed really badly, for his sister's dowry or his mother's operation, or whatever. I paid him double, because the concerto was so good, even though I knew the money would shorten his life (which it did; dead of liver failure at age twenty-six) and cheat the world of what he might have written. What can you do?

I'd reached the point where I couldn't play any more, so I packed up my flute and locked it away, made myself a last bowl of tea, and shuffled off to bed. I fell asleep straight away, and slipped into one of the old nightmares. Disappointing, because I hadn't been getting them since the delegation went home. I woke up in a sweat, and saw that the lamp was lit, and there was someone in the room with me.

She was eating an apple. I saw the lamplight reflected in her eyes. "Hello," she said.

I found it hard to breathe. "Are you going to kill me?" I asked.

"Silly," she said. "You'd be dead already."

I tried to sit up, but she frowned at me, so I stayed where I was. "You know who I am," she said.

"Yes," I replied. "I—" Words are useless. "I helped you once."

That made her laugh. She put down the apple on the bed, by my feet. "So I'm told," she said. "But I don't believe it. You're my father."

I nodded. "I guessed," I said.

"Because I have the same talent as you." She picked something up off the bed. It was a knife. One of mine, actually.

"How did you get past the guards?"

She smiled. "I feel sorry for them," she said. "But I guess they signed on of their own free will. They were in the way."

"You wiped their minds."

"Yes."

I was waiting for the tactical officer inside my head to suggest something, but nothing came. "That was a horrible thing to do."

"You've done worse."

"To save my life," I said. "I never tried to harm you."

"You had them put something nasty in my food," she replied, as though correcting an obvious flaw in my logic. "It didn't kill me, but it made me very ill. So I suggested, how would it be if we told everybody I died, and then he'd assume he'd succeeded, and I'd be safe. So that's what we did." She took another bite from the apple. "I gather you came to my funeral. Did you cry?"

"No."

She nodded. "I told them I wanted to stay behind, after they went home. I've got a few jobs to do while I'm here, and then I'll head back." She paused, as if waiting for something. "Why haven't you tried to get inside my head?"

"I wish you no harm," I told her.

"That's a good one." She took another bite from the

apple, then threw the core into the corner of the room. "You never mean any harm, do you? You didn't mean to blind your sister. Except you did. You held the branch back on purpose."

"How do you know that?"

She shrugged. "I know everything about you," she said. "More than you do."

"You've been inside my head."

Then she really laughed. She made a noise like a donkey. "You have no idea, have you? How much trouble you've caused. Well, of course you haven't, you saw to that. You ran away."

"People were trying to kill me."

"I don't mean *that*, stupid." She took a deep breath, then let it go slowly. "You know what," she said. "Once I made you a promise. I think I'll break it. Well? If I do, will you forgive me?"

I looked at her. "You never promised me anything."

"It's rude to call someone a liar. Well? Are you going to forgive me or not?"

I shrugged. "Does it matter?"

"Fine." She sat up straight, put down the knife, and folded her hands in her lap. "I made you a promise, about five years ago. You don't remember, do you?"

I shook my head.

"I came to see you," she said. "You don't remember,

but I do. You were living in a nice suite of rooms next door but two to the Old Theatre. There was a marble staircase, and a big oak door with a shutter in it. You had a servant, I think he was Cimbrian. You made him wear a white tunic with brass buttons." She paused and grinned at me. "Remember?"

"I remember."

"The big door opened into a sort of hall," she went on, "with a marble floor, white and red, in a chessboard pattern. There were three couches and a brass table. Oh, yes, and a sort of palm tree thing in a big clay pot. And you had a parrot, in a cage."

"Go on," I said.

"You were sitting on one of the couches, and you had a barber to shave you. He was a tall man with red hair, left-handed. His name was Euja, I know, because you said, Thank you, Euja, that's all for today. Remember?"

"Yes."

She nodded approvingly. "You told me to sit down and you rang a bell, for tea. It came in a red-and-white porcelain pot, and there was a dragon on the bottom of the bowl. Is that right?"

"Yes."

"You waited till the servant had poured the tea, then you asked me politely what you could do for me. You must've thought I was a customer. I was fifteen. I told you, I'm your daughter."

I stared at her—her eyes, not the side of her head. "Go on."

"I told you things about my mother, things I'd heard from the people who brought me up. They were servants from my mother's family. They died when I was six, in the plague, and the woman's sister had me then. But I told you things, about her, and you realised I was telling the truth."

"Go on."

She smiled at me. "I told you how poor we were, because all the money my mother's father left for me had gone. I knew you were rich. I asked you for money."

My mouth was dry. "What did I say?"

She frowned. "You looked at me for a long time. Then you asked how I'd found you. I said, I'd heard about you; how you could go inside people's heads and take away memories. That's how I knew. I could do it too. Of course," she went on, "I couldn't be sure until I told you the secret things, about my mother. You recognised them all, and then I was certain. But I made sure."

"You looked—"

"In your head, yes. I saw my mother's bedroom, just as my nurse described it. And anyway, I recognised you, from her memories. You were much younger then, of course. But your voice was the same."

My feet and knees had gone cold. "So," I said, "you asked me for money. What did I say?"

She was silent for a long time. "You said you wouldn't give me anything, but I could earn four thousand angels. If I'd do a simple job for you. Then you took a piece of paper from the brass table and wrote out a draft and showed it to me."

"I wanted you to take away a memory," I said. "Well?"

"Of course. What other possible use could I be?"

I closed my eyes. "What did you take from me?"

I heard her say, "This."

————————

I remembered it all, very clearly. I remembered hearing my younger sister crying, upstairs in the loft. I remember hearing my mother yelling at my father, the usual hateful stuff. Not again, I thought. I'd just come in from putting the chickens away; it was raining, and I was still wearing a coat, the big homespun that my uncle had left behind when he came to visit. I wanted to get to the fire—I was wet and cold—but that would mean going through the main room, which was where my mother and father were fighting. I decided I'd have to stay where I was until they stopped.

Then they came out past the chimney corner; I could

see them, but they hadn't seen me. My father staggered a little; I knew what that meant, he'd been drinking, and when he was drunk he did stupid things. I saw him reach in the corner for his stick, a heavy blackthorn cudgel I knew only too well. He took a step forward, and I knew he was about to hit my mother. She screamed at him, you're stupid, you're so stupid, I should have listened to my family, they said you were useless and you are. He swung at her, aiming for her head. Long practice made her duck and swerve, and he hit her on the arm. She tried to back away, but her foot caught in the rucked-up rug and she tripped forward, toward him. He was about to hit her again, and my inner tactician told me that this time he'd get her, because she was off-balance and couldn't get out of the way. I suddenly remembered that in my right hand was the knife I'd taken with me to cut the twine on the neck of the feed sack. I stepped forward, in between them, and whether my father walked into the knife or whether I stabbed him, I simply don't know.

My mother was staring at him. I'd let go of the knife; it was still stuck in him. He opened his mouth, but all that came out was blood. She grabbed the knife and pulled it out, and then he fell over, crushing the little table. Nobody falls like that unless they're dead.

She stood there for a moment or so, with the knife in her hand, looking at me; then I heard my sister's voice, up at the top of the ladder. My mother swung round and screamed, "Go to *bed*!"

I tried to say something, but I couldn't. I remember the look on her face. On the advice of my internal tactical officer I took a long step back, out of her reach.

He was going to kill you, I said.

Don't be so stupid, she snapped at me. He would never—

He hit you with the stick. He—

I remember her knuckles were white around the knife handle. I knew, in that moment; like me, inside her head was a little voice advising her on distances and angles, how long a step she'd need to take to reach me, how to drive the knife home without letting me parry or ward her off. I took two long strides back, then turned and ran—

———

"You paid me," she said, "to remove that. I've been keeping it safe for you all this time, like a trustee. I think you should have it back now."

I think I actually raised a hand in front of me. "No," I said. "Please, take it back. I don't think I could bear to live with it."

Then she grinned. "Oh, there's more," she said.

I remembered the day my father found my sister. He'd gone into the barn to get his billhook, and there she was, hanging from the crossbeam. He'd tried to cut her down, but in his shock and grief he'd cut himself to the bone; he ran into the house for something to bind the cut with, and I was there. Come with me, he shouted. I remembered seeing her. I remembered cutting her down, and how she landed like a hay bale tossed from the loft, and how he swore at me. I remembered the note she left, written on the flyleaf of the Book, because there was nothing else in the house to write on; how everybody hated her because she was so ugly, because of her missing eye. It was after that that my father started drinking.

I remembered the day I came home. I found my mother sitting in the kitchen. I remembered thinking how dirty the place was, not like it used to be, everything neat and clean. I got your letter, I told her.

She looked at me. I hadn't seen her since the night my father died, when she'd called out all the neighbours to look for me, because I'd murdered my father and ought to be hung.

I need you to do something for me, she said.

"That's enough," I said. "Whatever it is you think I've done to you, that's enough."

The girl gave me a quizzical look. "You killed my mother," she explained. "It's not nearly enough."

I need you to do something for me, she said.

I waited. It was as though she expected me to guess what it was. Well? I asked.

You can do that trick, she said. I've been hearing all about you. You're making ever so much money in the City.

If it's money, I said, but she scowled at me. You can take away memories.

Yes, I said.

Fine. I want you to go inside my mind and take out every memory of you. Everything. I want it so I don't know you ever existed. Can you do that? And your brother and sister too, I want them to forget you. Take it all away, then get out and never come back. That's all.

———————

"I think I may take after her," she said. "Strong. Single-minded."

"How the hell are you doing this?" I said. "I couldn't. I can only take them away, I can't put them back."

"I guess I'm better than you," she said. "Better than you in every way. That wouldn't be so hard." She raised an eyebrow. "Do you remember? How I came to you when I was fifteen, and all you wanted was to get rid of those memories? But you had money, and we needed it so badly. And you never told me—" She stopped for a moment. "You never told me what I was going to see. And I've had it inside me ever since. You forced it on me, like rape. I would never—"

"All right," I said. "So, what do you want me to do?"

Her eyes widened. "I want you to remember," she said.

———————

I remembered the letter. It was barely legible, written in cheap oak-gall ink on wrapping paper. This is to let you know, it said, that she died but the kid survived. Her father paid my husband and me to take the child away, but the money he gave us has all run out and we're poor and we need money. You have a daughter. She's five now. You can have her, if you like.

I remembered sending a draft for twenty angels, which was all I had; but I didn't go. I couldn't bear to. And I burned the letter, with the name and the address. Because I didn't want her daughter, I wanted—

————

"You never meant me to see that," she said. "But I did. And then you asked me to wipe me out of your mind as well, as though I'd never been born." She looked at me again. "How could you do that? Like mother, like son?"

I said, "I'll give you ten thousand angels. It's all I've got."

"I could get twice as much for you," she replied, "but then you'd die, and that'd be letting you off easy. And you're forgetting, you've got lots of money back in the City, with the Social and Beneficient. I want all that, as well."

I wrote her two drafts. She read them carefully, to make sure they were in order. Then she folded them and tucked them into her sleeve. "What's so sad about it," she said, "is that all the really bad things you ever did were done for love—killing your father and my mother,

I mean, blinding your sister was just stupid. You're really very stupid, aren't you? That's what your mother called your father." She examined me, as if she were considering buying me. "Are you happy?" she said. "Now, I mean. Here and now."

"Yes," I said. "Or I was."

She tutted. "Can't have that," she said. "I think that playing the flute's given you more happiness than anything else in your life, and that was someone else's, wasn't it? I don't think you can be allowed to keep it. I think I'll have it instead."

I felt the burning pain, just above my ear. "Sorry," she said. "Actually, I can do it without hurting, but it takes a little bit more effort, and I couldn't be bothered. Don't worry," she went on, "you can still remember what it was like being a famous musician. I've just taken what you took. That's fair, isn't it?"

Instinctively, I tried to remember how to hold a flute, how you shape your lips, the spread of the fingers. All gone. I had no idea.

"I remember wondering," she was saying, "why you didn't have me wipe my mother out of your head. Those memories must've been painful, but you kept them. No, don't explain," she added, "I'd like to think it was some last spark of decency in you, and anything you say will probably disappoint me. I don't want to have to punish you any more than I have already. I'm not a cruel person, you understand. It's just that you disgust me so much. I wish you were a spider, so I could squash you."

I looked at her; at the spot just above her ugly, lobeless ear. "What else can you do?" I said. "Apart from memories."

She grinned. "Oh, lots of things. I can put ideas in people's heads—like, for instance, I once met a really nasty man who had this special talent that allowed him to make stupid amounts of money. So I gave him this urge to gamble it all away. That's justice, don't you think?"

I shook my head. "That wasn't you."

"Maybe. Maybe not. How could you ever know for sure?" She laughed. "And now I think it's time you did something for me. Call it twenty years' worth of birthday presents from my father."

I remember—I don't know whose memory it was, mine or someone else's—the time I got beaten up in the dockyards, late at night. I think it must've been me, because it was over some trivial gambling debt. I remember the point where they were still hitting me, but I'd stopped feeling it, and I was just bone weary, I wanted to lie down and go to sleep but they wouldn't let me.

"Let me guess," I said.

So I went into her mind, and there she was standing over me while I took down the scrolls from the shelves, watching to make sure I didn't stick my nose in to anything else while I was there. Then I remembered going to see *me,* how badly I treated her, as though she had some horrible contagious disease. Then she pushed me out again; I found myself back in my bed, and she was staring at me.

I took a deep breath. "It's all right," I said. "Nothing bad's happened. Just go home."

She frowned. "Did I know you?" she said.

"No," I told her. "Don't lose the bits of paper in your sleeve, they're valuable. Don't think about anything. Just go home."

Which she did; and so did I, back to the City, where I belonged.

Not straightaway, of course. I got my friend the director to arrange for me to be smuggled safely over the border; then I walked (no money, remember?) all the way to the City. I was scared stiff I'd be recognised, but luckily I didn't run into anybody who remembered me. I went to the house where the old man and his son lived. I feel guilty about what I did to their guards and some of the servants, but they were in the way. I feel no guilt at all about what I did to the old man and his son.

Very soon afterwards, the new regime collapsed—as was inevitable, with its two leading lights reduced to vegetables. A few months later, they held proper elections again. After the inauguration of the new Consul and his cabinet, there was a grand reception at the Palace; entertainment was provided by a talented young flautist. Nobody knows where she suddenly appeared from, but people who should know compare her favourably with Clamanzi at his best. I've followed her career with interest, though from a distance; I've never actually heard her play. People who know her say that's she's happy, completely caught up in her music. I'm glad about that.

Of course, I don't live in the City these days. I moved to Permia, bought a large farm, I'm completely retired now. In case you're wondering: before I left the City, I stole a spade and went to a place on the moors, south of town, and dug up a big steel box full of gold coins. I knew where to look for it, thanks to the clerk who stole it from the old man and his son—I never break a professional confidence, but I don't always tell the truth. No angel, you might say. Ah, well.

I don't want to detain you any longer than necessary, but I'd just like to share a few insights with you, as the world's greatest living authority on suffering. I reckon I can claim that honour. I've caused more suffering, endured more suffering, witnessed, experienced, inflicted, savoured, analysed, enjoyed, dissected, wallowed in more suffering than anybody else who's ever lived. I have been in the mind of my enemy, my victim, my persecutor, your enemy, your victim, your persecutor; I know pain like fish know water, like birds know air. Suffering has fed and clothed me most of my life, I've sunk my roots deep into it and sucked it up into me; pain and suffering have made me what I am. To be quite honest, I'm sick and tired of it.

Along the way, I guess I've lost my edge a bit—like blacksmiths, whose fingertips get burned so much they lose the fine touch. I'm not sure I can tell whose pain is which any more; is the child crying in the street me or just some stranger? Answer: to make a distinction is to miss the point entirely. To try and rationalise all this in terms of right, wrong, good, evil, is just naïve; the very worst things we do, after all, we do for love, and the very worst pain we feel comes from love. She was right about that. In my opinion, love is the greatest and most enduring enemy, because love gives rise to the memories that kill us, slowly, every day. I think a man who never encounters love might quite possibly live forever. He'd have to, because if he died, who the hell would ever remember him?

About the Author

Photograph by Shelley Humphries

Having worked in journalism, numismatics, and the law, K. J. Parker now writes for a precarious living.

K. J. Parker also writes under the name Tom Holt.

TOR·COM

Science fiction. Fantasy.
The universe.
And related subjects.

*

More than just a publisher's website, Tor.com
is a venue for **original fiction, comics,** and
discussion of the entire field of SF and fantasy,
in all media and from all sources. Visit our site
today—and join the conversation yourself.

CPSIA information can be obtained at www.ICGtesting.com
Printed in the USA
LVOW06s1738021115

460765LV00002B/134/P